Clare Connelly was ra~~
amongst a family of av~~
of her childhood up a tr~~
hand. Clare is married ~~
and they live in a bungalow near the sea with their
two children. She is frequently found staring into
space—a sure-fire sign that she's in the world of her
characters. She has a penchant for French food and
ice-cold champagne, and Mills & Boons continue
to be her favourite ever books. Writing for Mills &
Boon is a long-held dream. Clare can be contacted via
clareconnelly.com or her Facebook page.

If you liked *Off Limits*, why not try

A Week to be Wild by JC Harroway
Legal Seduction by Lisa Childs
Ruled by Anne Marsh

Discover more at millsandboon.co.uk

OFF LIMITS

CLARE CONNELLY

MILLS & BOON

First Published in Great Britain 2018
by Mills & Boon, an imprint of HarperCollins*Publishers*
1 London Bridge Street, London, SE1 9GF

© 2018 Clare Connelly

ISBN: 978-0-263-93205-8

MIX
Paper from
responsible sources
FSC® C007454

This book is produced from independently certified FSC™ paper
to ensure responsible forest management.
For more information visit www.harpercollins.co.uk/green.

Printed and bound in Spain
by CPI, Barcelona

This book is for romance readers everywhere,
who fall in love again and again with the characters
of our creation.

You give our stories life just by reading them.

Thank you.

PROLOGUE

The stars are not wanted now: put out every one;
Pack up the moon and dismantle the sun;
Pour away the ocean and sweep up the wood.
For nothing now can ever come to any good.
　　　　　　　　　　　　　　　　—WH Auden

'YOU'VE GOT THE Prime Minister calling in ten minutes.'

Jack nods, showing not a flicker of response at the prospect of this. Then again, nothing about Jack Grant is what you'd expect. For a self-made billionaire-investor-cum-philanthropist-cum-sex-god, he is wild, disrespectful of authority and the establishment, and rough around the edges. Deliciously so.

Take this situation: Jack, in his bed, naked as the day he was born, uncaring that he should have been at his desk an hour ago. That I can see most of his beautiful back and backside. That my insides are clenching with hot, steamy lust.

'About...?'

It's a lazy drawl as he flips over and pierces me with those intelligent green eyes. His accent is pure Irish brogue. Like Colin Farrell after a night of cigarettes and booze: deep, hoarse and throaty.

'The latest episode of *The Great British Bake Off*.'

I roll my eyes. We've been negotiating to buy a huge swathe of Crown land for the last six months; it's at the highest level of negotiation and, given the media interest, the Prime Minister has become involved.

'What do you *think*?'

His laugh is a rumble that barrels out of his chest. 'Well, every man needs a good scone recipe.'

'And you've got one?'

'Sure.'

He grins. It's a grin that is at once devilish and charming, and I know how easy it must be for him to get women into bed. And that's before you factor in the body, the money, the power.

'Nine minutes,' I snap.

His grin unfurls like a ribbon on his face. My heart *kerthunks*. I ignore it. Stupid heart.

'Did you book Sydney?'

'Yes.'

He arches a brow at my impatient tone and, as if to contradict it, stretches in the bed, his arms high over his head, his body gloriously on display for me.

'And, Amber?'

I don't mean to sigh but when the Prime Minister's office is calling I feel there should be some air of responsiveness. Jack, apparently, doesn't agree.

'All arranged.'

Lucy's sister is taking a year's sabbatical from her job as an executive at a bank to manage the foundation's start-up year. She's insanely qualified and personally motivated.

'Salary agreed; she'll be based out of Edinburgh, as we discussed.'

He nods, but makes no effort to move.

'Seriously, Jack. Eight minutes. Get the hell up, already.'

'Ouch. Did you get out of the wrong side of bed this morning?'

He runs his fingers down his chest, drawing my attention to the ridges of his abdomen, the flesh so perfectly smooth and sculpted. My mouth is bone-dry.

'No.'

'You're even crosser than usual,' he teases, and my lips tighten impatiently.

As it happens, he's right. I got The Invitation this morning. The one that arrives every year, beckoning me to come and pay homage to my parents' marriage.

Ugh.

It's my least favourite social event—and the one time I'm forced to remember who I really am. The one time a year my parents recall me to the mother ship, reminding me that no matter what I do, professionally or personally, I'll always be Gemma Picton. *Lady* Gemma Picton.

Ugh.

'Sit down. Tell me all about it.'

He pats the bed beside him and I roll my eyes again, hoping he won't know how sorely I'm tempted. Just once I imagine giving in to *this*—the electrical current that is arcing between us. I never would…never could. He is as off-limits as hell is hot—the stuff of fantasies and nightmares.

'No, thanks.'

'What is it?'

'Nothing. Personal stuff,' I say, and he shrugs.

But there's curiosity in his eyes. A curiosity I have to ignore. Along with desire. Lust. Want. Need.

We have our boundaries and we definitely know better than to cross them.

Jack pushes the sheet off, exposing the tattoo that curls across his lower back and snakes around his hips to the tops of his legs. It must have hurt like hell to get it done—especially on the skin of his thighs, right near his cock.

I asked him once why he'd got it. His answer? *'Seemed like a good idea at the time.'*

He doesn't care that I see him naked. It's not the first time and undoubtedly won't be the last. Sometimes I wonder if he's goading me, waiting for me to react. After all, it's classic workplace sexual harassment.

Except it isn't. Because I'm not harassed.

I'm amused. And more than a little turned on.

In the two years since I started working for Jack I've probably seen him naked on average once per week. That's over a hundred stare-fests and he is *totally* worth staring at. I don't think he used to be like this. Before *this* there was *her*.

Lucy.

His wife.

But she got sick and died, and two months later I came to work for him and he was like this. Dark and brooding and desirable and sexy and messed up and mourning and fascinating.

This sleeping with anything in a skirt is post-Lucy. Same as the copious Scotch-drinking afterwards. It's sensual self-flagellation but he won't see it that way.

So, no matter how much I want to stare at his naked arse, I know he's for looking at—not touching. Like when Grandma used to take me shopping at her favourite Portmeirion boutique and I was allowed to stare at the intricate floral and botanical artwork for hours on end, but never, ever to touch.

Because touching might lead to breaking—and, yes, touching Jack would, I fear, break me.

'See something you like?'

Another drawl—he's so good at that. He lets words slide out of his mouth like liquid chocolate.

'Nope.' My smile is saccharine. 'Seven minutes.'

I spin on my heel and leave, a smile playing around my lips as desire pools between my legs.

Gemma is staring at me, and the mood I'm in I feel about two steps away from going all 'Me Tarzan, You Jane' on her. I want to grab her round the waist and pull her down on my length. No foreplay. No teasing. Just her…taking me deep.

In my fantasy she's not wearing panties and she's left her brain at the door—because real-life Gemma would quote me a thousand reasons not to have sex even as she was moaning in my arms.

Last night was fun. At least, it started off as fun. But the woman I brought here…Rebecca? Rowena?… talked too much.

She'd wanted to be romanced.

I wanted to screw.

So I gave her cab fare and showed her the door.

And now I have a raging hard-on and an assistant— she hates it when I call her that, so I do it often, even though she's technically my in-house counsel—who seems to have moved into my sexual fantasies permanently. When did *that* happen?

I rack my brain, trying to pinpoint the moment I went from observing her to obsessing over her. From looking dispassionately at her in those suits she wears one day, and the next imagining how long it would take me to strip her out of one.

I don't think it was one *day*, though, because that implies some switch was flicked. No, I think it was a look as she got into my helicopter in Spain. A laugh over dinner. Hearing her hum as she stared out of a window, her mind obviously running at a million miles an hour.

Then there was that blackout we were once caught in at the City office. The fire alarm shut the place down, closing us inside an elevator for close on an hour, with just the dim flicker of emergency lights that made her legs look so long and smooth. By the time they cranked the doors I was about ready to pin her to the carpeted floor and screw her senseless.

Yeah, that was probably the moment I realised how much trouble I was in.

I'm not interested in a relationship. But I do want to fuck her. And I think she wants it, too. I've seen the way her caramel eyes drop to my arse when she thinks I'm not looking.

But I'm always looking lately.

CHAPTER ONE

SHE MIGHT AS well be naked. The dress is skin-tight, bright red and low-cut. Tiny straps slip over her shoulders. The dress is short, too. Not indecently short but, *Jesus*, her legs are long and smooth, and while she's wearing that dress I find it impossible to look away.

She's hotter than any woman here—and that's saying something, given that this launch event has brought together most of London's elite. There are models, actresses, singers, athletes, and lots of those women who've married for money and now make it their life's work to live up to their husbands' expectations.

And then there's Gemma.

Her blond hair is pulled into a ballerina bun, her face is serious and her body is like pale silk that I want to wrap around me.

She's said something funny, going by the way the guy with her leans forward and laughs. Is he her date? A frown pulls at my brow. I stare harder. Did she bring a date? Isn't she technically here as my plus-one?

Seeing her with another guy does something dangerous to my equilibrium. A possessive impulse threads through me, knotting at my chest.

I pull a couple of champagne flutes from a passing

waiter and cut through the room. I'm aware of people trying to get my attention but I have no time for them. Gemma is in my sights.

'Jack…'

Her lips purse as I approach; her eyes flick to me in that way she has. How is it possible for one person to imbue a simple gesture with a measure of cold disdain even when there's the hint of a smile somewhere in that symmetrical face of hers?

I hand her a glass of champagne and she takes it, her fingers briefly wrapping over mine. Immediately my mind puts them elsewhere on my body.

'You remember Wolf DuChamp?' she says. 'He manages our accounts in New York.'

I remember his stupid name, but not the man himself. Nothing memorable about blond, pretty-boy looks and that air of Ivy League he seems to wear like a coat.

'Sure.' I extend my hand, knowing I have to meet the convention even when my body is singularly focussed on Gemma.

'Good to see you again, sir.'

Gemma's lips quiver. I hate being called 'sir' and she knows it. Out of nowhere I have an image of her saying it to me, bent at the knees, her eyes moving up my body to meet mine as her lips clamp down on my length. Okay, maybe in some circumstances I could make an exception…

What the hell am I thinking? These fantasies are one thing, but screwing Gemma cannot happen.

Cannot happen. Might as well get that tattoo added to my collection.

'I was just explaining the software overhaul we're looking at to Gem.'

Is he trying to piss me off? First of all by removing the very nice image I was enjoying by talking about software. And then by referring to Gemma as 'Gem'—as though they're best buddies who paint their nails together.

'I'll summarise it for you later,' she says, sensing my impatience though I suspect not the reason for it.

'It'll make a huge difference to our operations,' Wolf pushes.

'Gem' angles her body a bit, turning away from me, giving me a chance to escape.

'I'll look into the feasibility. The problem is going to be short-term. We'll need to make sure the systems are protected during the transfer of data. You handle some of our most sensitive work—a data breach would be unacceptable.'

'I've thought of that, too,' Wolf carries on—and I am dismissed, it would appear.

Across the room a platinum blonde with a sensational rack and legs that go on forever is trying to catch my eye.

I want Gemma, but I can't have her. And I'm not one to wallow in self-pity. There's plenty of fish in the sea.

I have two rules when it comes to the women I fuck.

No commitment.

No redheads.

Commitment was for Lucy.

And Lucy was a redhead.

I freeze. A vision of Lucy is in front of me, a scowl of disapproval on her face. I messed around a fair bit before we met, but nothing like this. I've taken it to a whole new level and I don't care. Except for that scowl. Even in death I don't want to upset Lucy.

What did you expect, Luce? You left me a pretty big void to fill.

Don't blame me, I hear her snap back. *Your life. Your choice.*

Yeah, right.

My eyes wander of their own accord back to Gemma. She's got her head bent now, and Wolf's fingers are typing something into his cell phone. She nods and smiles, then presses a hand to his forearm. My stomach rolls on a surge of emotion I don't much care for.

I stalk towards the blonde as though she is the only woman in the room.

'I'm Jack Grant.'

Her lips are painted a bright red. She purrs. 'I know who you are.'

'Then you have the advantage.'

Her lips part. 'From what I hear, telling you my name wouldn't serve much purpose. You won't remember it tomorrow, right?'

I laugh, appreciating her honesty. 'No…' I lean forward so that my lips are only a whisper from her ear. My breath flutters her hair and I see a fine trail of goose bumps run across her skin. 'But you'll remember *me* for the rest of your life.'

Her laugh is husky. She's everything I would usually find sexy, but in that moment she's just passably acceptable. If I'm honest, I'm bored. It's a phone-it-in flirt. A *What the heck?* situation.

'We'll see…'

'Can I get you a drink?'

'I can share yours,' she murmurs, her eyes dropping to my champagne flute.

I didn't even realise I was still holding it. I extend

it to her on autopilot, watching as her lips shape over the glass and she tilts it back. The liquid is honey-gold. She passes the glass to me and I take a sip.

'Let's get out of here,' she says, with a throaty laugh in the rushed words.

I nod, reaching down and putting a hand in the small of her back. Gemma and Lucy are both in my head now—a fascinating occurrence. A *new* occurrence. Are they ganging up on me? Would they even *like* each other?

Lucy was so soft and sweet. She looked at me like I was her saviour and I suppose I was. I ripped her out of her old life, away from a boyfriend who used her as a punching bag, and I made all her dreams come true.

But fate is a bastard of a thing, and it only had bad news in store for Lucy. For a while she managed to jump tracks and sit on a different train, and then— *bam*. It took her. You can't outrun destiny, can you?

Gemma is nothing like her. Her personality isn't so much hard edges as a single hard face. She is smart— smarter than me by a mile—and focussed in a way that is completely familiar to me. She is also sexy. I don't know how I know that, but I do. She acts so damned cold around me—as though she's never so much as *heard* of an orgasm, much less experienced one. It makes me want her more. Want to show her for the liar she is. To make her orgasm again and again until 'cold' is a very distant memory.

'Jack.'

She catches me as I'm about to leave the room. Her eyes briefly meet the blonde's. There is nothing beyond a polite acknowledgement of her existence. That iciness is there. I want to push Gemma backwards against the wall and kiss the hell out of her. Right here.

'You're scheduled to speak in twenty minutes.'

Whoops. Even for me that's a bit of a slip. I don't usually let anything get in the way of business—even my sex life.

'We'll be back by then.'

Blondie surprises us both. Her meaning is unmistakable.

Shit. I can't remember the last time I had a quickie in the car. Is she seriously suggesting it?

Gemma shifts her attention to her phone. She runs that iPhone as though she designed the thing. Her fingers fly over the screen like it's a part of her. Her complacency pisses me off.

'Okay. The talk can be brief. Just an outline of what the foundation is hoping to achieve, thanking the commercial partners, yada-yada-yada.'

'Yada-yada-yada?' I grin slowly, my eyes linking with hers, daring her to forget the coldness and complacency.

She looks at Blondie and her smile is perfunctory. 'Have fun.'

Of course Jack nails the speech. Not so much as a hair on his head looks out of place. The tuxedo is immaculate. The white shirt crisp. The bow tie in place as though glued. He speaks eloquently about the foundation and he also speaks with humour, so the crowd laughs.

I don't.

I am wondering about the blonde.

No. I'm thinking about Jack—but they're thoughts that I need to run a mile from. This *can't* control me.

I've worked my arse off in this job, twisting myself in mental knots to stay on top of my workload without breaking a sweat, and I am *not* going to let the fact that my boss is impossibly hot get in the way.

Instead I let my attention drift to Wolf.

He's talking to someone else now—no doubt about that bloody software. His face is serious, and that makes me smile. Because Wolf is pretty much always serious.

Warning! Warning! Warning! It flashes inside my mind. Because I don't *do* serious, and if I let the flirtation with Wolf keep going I think he's going to see roses and candy and wedding bells.

God help me, I can't think of anything worse.

I am suffocating at the very *idea* of being a bride in white, having Wolf waiting for me at the end of an aisle. He would definitely want children, too. Three of them. And he'd expect me to be the obliging baby-maker and carer. He'd look at me with those puppy-dog eyes, sadness and disappointment on his features, if I so much as dared suggest we get a nanny.

Maybe I could be like Marissa Mayer and have a nursery built into my office? The nanny could be based there, so I could still be one of those hands-on Pinterest-type mummies. Wolf would never even need to know I'd hired someone to help.

But Jack would. He'd *hate* that. A baby crying when I'm trying to talk to him about tariffs on our Chinese imports? No, he'd probably seduce the nanny and then I'd have to either fire her or kill her.

Okay, *now* who's getting ahead of themselves?

But Wolf has caught me watching him and his heart is so on his sleeve he might as well be a cartoon character, with one of those thought bubbles popping out of his head. I *have* to let this opportunity pass me by. He's not right, and when he realises that I'm not going to leave Jack and move to Manhattan, working with him will become a nightmare.

I look away.

Right at Jack.

He's standing in front of me.

The band has started to play and I've been so lost in imagining the hell of my future with Wolf DuChamp that I haven't realised.

'Did you like the speech?'

'Looking for compliments?' I sip my champagne, pleased at how quickly I'm able to recover. 'What's the matter? Wasn't she suitably impressed?'

His eyes clash with mine. He's angry. *Ooooh.* Why? Have I hit the nail on the head somehow?

'Are you wondering if I can please a woman in fifteen minutes?'

He shifts his body infinitesimally, but enough to spark something low in my abdomen. Anger. Resentment. Heat. Warmth. Need.

Fuck.

'Believe it or not, I haven't given any thought to your bedroom prowess,' I lie, shifting my attention back to the room of people. London's elite swirl around us, and I am wanting to swirl away with them.

'Liar,' he says, so softly I think I've misheard.

Because we can't go there! He knows that—I know that. Every bone in my body wants him, but my brain is still in charge. I don't want to screw up my career, but it's more than that. I *love* Jack. Not in *that* way. I mean I love working with him. Even when he's at his assholiest, he's become one of the biggest constants in my life. How stupid would it be to rock the boat?

I imagine, briefly, that we indulge in an affair and it ends—because Jack doesn't do permanent—and then I imagine not seeing him again.

It makes me ill.

I don't want to think about it.

I don't want to risk it.

'The speech was good.' I bring the conversation back onto far safer ground, trying to fold my desperate realisations away neatly into a box I won't open again.

'Tell me something, Gemma,' he says, and the tone of his voice is still dangerous to me.

He hasn't got my silent memo, obviously, because his words prick the blood in my veins until it gushes and gurgles through me—he's flirting with me.

I use my most businesslike tone. 'Oh, I don't know if you really want me to do that. You might not like what I say...'

His eyes lance mine. It's like being sliced through.

'What's the deal with you and that guy from New York?'

Who's he talking about? Oh. Right. 'You mean Wolf?'

His lips curl derisively—that's one of my favourite of his expressions. I don't know if he realises how devilishly sexy he looks.

'Who calls their kid after an *animal*? Especially when he's the least wolf-like person you can imagine.'

'I don't suppose they knew that when he was born,' I say, but a smile is pushing at my lips. He's right. Wolf is handsome, but in a very neat and tidy kind of way.

'Is he a wolf in the bedroom?'

The question catches me completely off guard. It's

wholly new territory for us. Invasive in a way I don't know if I like but am worried that I might.

Still, challenging Jack is what I do. That's who we are.

I tilt my head to one side, assessing him for a moment, before volleying back, 'How was the blonde?'

'She was dull,' he says with a shrug and no hesitation, apparently having no qualms discussing his sex-life with me.

'Where is she?'

'At her house. Waiting.'

'For you?'

He shrugs. 'I said I might stop by. It seemed like the only way to get rid of her.'

Wait. He *hasn't* slept with her? No, not slept with. Fucked. The thought is oddly elating, though I can't help but feel sympathy for the woman he flirted with and then sent packing.

'You really are a bastard,' I mutter. 'Are you going to go to her?'

His eyes are probing mine now, and I feel like every single one of my fantasies, my dirtiest, hottest dreams, are playing out between us like a kinky Pensieve for his pleasure.

Yes, I'm a Harry Potter diehard. Hermione was one of my first role models.

'Maybe.'

My stomach turns. I am used to this feeling with Jack. In the first six months we worked together I wasn't so adept at dealing with his vivid love-life. I blushed whenever I found evidence of his nocturnal activities, and I couldn't always meet his eye. But now? Well, now I've had two years to practise acceptance.

I smile blandly. 'Well…' I shrug as though my

heart's not racing and my nipples aren't throbbing. 'Have a good night.'

'Wait.' His words are commanding, and so too is the hand he clamps around my wrist.

I jerk my face towards his, the breath exploding out of me. We *don't* touch. No more than an accidental brush of fingers from time to time. That's impossible to avoid when you're together as often as we are.

Definitely not like this.

His thumb pads across my inner wrist, and when I don't say anything he pulls me, hard and fast, so that my body rams into his. We are surrounded and yet we are alone. There is a void that engulfs us. Like a sensual electric fence.

This is all new and all wrong. And so right.

His body is tight. Hard. Hot. Just as it is in all my fantasies. It takes every single ounce of my willpower to close my mouth and let my breath return to normal. To look at him as though he's lost his mind, not made me lose mine.

'Yes, sir?'

His eyes flare. I meant it to put him back on his guard, to remind him of the boundaries of our relationship, but I might as well have struck a match over gasoline. He doesn't let me go.

'Dance with me.'

The air around us is charged with expectation and I just know he's asking for more than a dance. Does he expect me to say no? I don't like living up to expectations, and I'm not going to give him a reason to think I'm afraid of what's going on between us.

'Fine.' My smile is tight. It stretches over my face like sunburn.

He expels a breath, long and slow, and places a hand in the small of my back. No...just at the very top of my arse. His fingers are splayed wide and they press into me firmly, so that I'm propelled towards him. His other hand links with my fingers, wrapping through them.

I focus on the band, my eyes taking in the details of their appearance while I concentrate on looking completely calm. I'm not, though. I'm weak when I want to be strong, and I need something that I shouldn't.

'This dress is sensational,' he says, immediately shattering my attempts to find calm.

'Is that your informed fashion opinion?'

Too tart. I soften the snap with a smile. It's a mistake. His eyes are mocking, his own smile sardonic.

I look away again immediately.

'It's my informed opinion as a red-blooded male.'

'What do you like about it?'

Warning lights are flashing in my mind, clamouring for attention. They are bright and angry. What am I *doing*?

'Let me see,' he murmurs. 'The colour. The way it's literally glued to your skin.'

He drops his head closer and heat spirals inside me; my blood is a vapour of steam in my veins.

This isn't right. It's not us. He sleeps with other women and, sure, he flirts the heck out of me, but that's harmless.

This doesn't feel harmless.

The music slows and I slow with it, putting some space between us with what I tell myself is relief.

'Get me up to speed on the New York situation,' he says.

'I intend to.'

I'm snappy because I'm uncertain. I'm completely wrong-footed by his nearness, his touch, and my own desire for him is swamping me. I need a minute to re-group, but his fingers are giving me no time. They're throbbing across my spine, my arse, and I am heating up by the second.

'Tonight. Now.'

I angle my head towards Wolf unconsciously. He's still locked in conversation. I have no intention of going home with him, and yet I resent Jack's implication that I don't have a life of my own.

'It's not urgent.' My words are stiff. 'It'll keep till tomorrow.' And I force myself to pull completely free of Jack's grip.

It's the equivalent of grabbing a lifeline from the side of a sinking boat. It's slippery, and I'm pretty sure I'm not strong enough to hold on to it for long enough to save myself. Drowning is inevitable.

'I want to hear about it tonight.'

It's a challenge. A gauntlet. He gives me a lot of latitude in my job because he knows how much I do. And I do it well. But at the end of the day he's my boss, and I don't know if anything is to be served by refusing him this request.

'Fine,' I say with a shrug of my shoulders. But I'm not going to let him think he's won. 'I just need... twenty minutes.'

I disconnect myself from him and try not to register how my body screams in frustration.

I saunter off towards Wolf before I can see if Jack's reacting in the same way.

Wolf is deep in conversation when I approach. 'May

I have a moment?' I look with a hint of apology towards the men he's with.

'Sure.' He grins at me. A nice grin. He really is good to look at. Not groundbreaking, earth-shattering, but *nice*.

He puts a hand on my elbow but I am leading *him*, walking quickly out of the ballroom, seeking privacy for no reason other than to give Jack a taste of his own damned medicine. That and to send a loud and clear message. He doesn't control every part of me.

'All good for later?' Wolf asks.

I smile. 'No, it's not. I have to work tonight, actually. I'm going to brief Jack on the software situation.'

'Tonight?' He arches a brow, his voice rich with disbelief.

'He micromanages *everything*,' I explain. It's true. 'And he's impatient as hell. I just want to make sure I have all the information.'

He nods, not quite hiding his disappointment. 'Let's recap.'

And that's how I spend the nineteen minutes I have. Well, eighteen… I allow myself one minute to pull a bit of my hair loose from its bun and to pinch my cheeks, making them appear flushed with pleasure.

Jack is waiting for me in the limousine twenty-five minutes after I left him. I imitate breathlessness as I step inside, and enjoy the way his eyes sweep over me with undisguised speculation.

'Ready?'

It's not what I expected. I nod, but as I do so I feel like maybe I'm agreeing to something I don't understand. Like there's a hidden meaning I don't yet know.

'Yeah. Let's go.'

CHAPTER TWO

I'LL SAY THIS for Jack. He knows how to do *this*. Late-night entertaining is clearly his forte.

His office is dimly lit and he's switched on some kind of acoustic guitar album that's humming low in my abdomen. The vocalist has a husky rasp and it's doing very strange things to my equilibrium. He mixes two martinis with a maraschino cherry in each.

I arch a brow as he hands me mine. 'I hate cherries.'

'Interesting,' he murmurs, his eyes hooked to mine. 'Why?'

I stare at it and swirl the glass, sipping the alcohol and wincing as the slightly medicinal flavour assaults my back palette. 'They're weird. Plasticky.'

'Not the real ones.'

'No.'

I swallow, wondering at the way my gut is churning and my pulse is racing. I need to bring it back to business. It's the reason I'm here with him.

'The server in Canada can pick up the slack, but it's going to slow things down.'

'By how much?'

'Just a few seconds' lag. It's unavoidable, given the distance.'

'A few seconds?' He shakes his head. 'There's nowhere closer?'

'Not that can handle this amount of data.'

He throws his drink back in one motion. 'And *Wolf* thinks that's acceptable?'

He says his name with obvious derision.

'You think he'd go to the effort of flying out here to propose it if he did?'

'Well, he's banging you, right?'

I can't hide the angry intake of breath. Sure, he's always rude. And demanding. And I've learned not to give a shit. I don't expect the same courtesy from Jack Grant that most people pepper into life. But this is too far even for him...even when we've been flirting all night.

'His suggestion is professional,' I return softly. A warning lurks in my words. Does he hear it?

Apparently not. Jack is like a cat with a mouse.

'But you are fucking him?'

'God, Jack,' I snap, standing up.

His eyes follow the fluidity of my movement. They're narrowed. Assessing. He's reading me like a book. But I'm too angry to care. Too worked up, as well. He's halfway to being drunk, and he's obnoxious, and since he pulled me hard against his body I'm a bit mushy.

I hide my mushiness, though. I hide it behind a veil of anger. 'That's none of your damned business.'

His eyes flick to mine. There's a lazy arrogance in his features but anger palpitates off him.

'He works for me. You work for me. If you're fucking him I want to know.'

'What I do in my own time, and with whom, is up

to me. Until the day it starts affecting my job performance you should just butt out.' I jut my chin, my eyes sparking with his. 'Got it?'

He looks calm, controlled, but I know there's an undercurrent of emotion just beneath the handsome surface. Because I know Jack. Probably better than anyone else on earth.

'You don't strike me as coy,' he says.

'Because I'm not.'

I step backwards. The wall is behind me. I brush against it, feeling cornered and unbelievably confused and turned on by this strange turn of events.

'So answer the question.'

'Am I fucking Wolf?' My question emerges as a husk in the night.

'Yeah.' He moves forward. An infinitesimal step. 'You know everything there is to know about me, don't you? So why keep your secrets?'

I open my mouth to say something snappy, but shut it again. He's right. I know a lot about him. Not the 'everything' he claims, but a lot.

'You could always lock your door if you want to be more private about your love-life.'

'*Sex*-life,' he interjects swiftly, on autopilot, and I know it's because of Lucy that he's so emphatic on this point.

I don't know anything about his wife. I presume she was a nice enough person—although agreeing to marry Jack does make me question both her sanity and her judgement. But maybe he was different before she died. Maybe his bastard impulses weren't so apparent?

'So you're going to live out the rest of your life like this? Moving from one woman to another, never getting to know a thing about them beyond their cup size and their sexual proclivities.'

His eyes drop to my breasts and I can tell he is assessing *my* cup size. *Crap.* My nipples strain hard against the flimsy fabric of my dress—it's too tight for a bra, and sadly I don't really need one.

His smile is self-satisfied and I want to slap it off his face. I fight the urge to cross my arms and cover my involuntary reaction.

'I'm trying to get to know more about you right now,' he says.

My pulse is hammering hard in my veins. His revolving-door bedroom flashes before me in an instant. The number of mornings I've arrived to find him asleep after a busy night of... Best I don't imagine that right now.

'Are you afraid I'll judge you?'

I open my eyes to find him right in front of me, his head bent, his body just a hair's breadth from me. A soft moan escapes me before I can catch it.

'You? You think you'd have any right to judge me after parading half of England through here?'

'Not half of *England*,' he murmurs, a smile shifting over his face. 'Half of London, maybe.'

'How do you justify it?' I ask, feeling a dangerous pull towards a line of questioning my brain is shouting at me to back away from. 'You think Lucy would be happy that you're fucking your way through a smorgasbord of women just because you won't have an actual relationship? Is there a sliding scale of monogamy that the dead expect?'

A muscle jerks in his cheek. I recognise that I'm stirring him up and still I don't stop. I'm angry, too!

He doesn't have a monopoly on thwarted desire and pent-up frustration.

It feels good to goad him! *So* good!

'You think what you do is fair to these women?'

His smile spreads slowly, but it is cold, angry. 'I don't hear any complaints.'

Boom! It's the proverbial match to the fuel of my anger. I explode.

'You boot them out before you even know their names half the time! Where, exactly, would they lodge their complaint? My God, Jack. Of all the chauvinistic, selfish, careless—'

He lifts a finger to my lips, silencing me with the touch. His eyes on mine are intent. Heat builds inside my blood, at fever pitch now.

'You know…' His fingers dip into my drink, fishing out the bright red orb at its base. 'You have a tendency to be judgemental.'

My sharp intake of breath is dangerous, given his finger's closeness to my mouth. He runs it across my lower lip and I don't pull away. He holds up the cherry with his other hand. My eyes slip to it of their own accord.

'Haven't you ever discovered that you like something you thought you hated? Haven't you ever been wrong?'

I shake my head, not really sure of the question he's asking. He surprises me by lifting the cherry to his own lips and sucking it into his mouth. I watch for a moment, and as his finger drops from my mouth I try to say something. I'm not sure what, and I'll never have a chance to find out. He brings his lips to mine, pressing the cherry into my mouth, rolling it around before sucking it back into his and crushing it.

The flavour is all around me and I no longer care. Because it is dwarfed by something else: the taste of *him*. Cherry flavour is on his tongue, evaporating in the flame of our kiss.

His lips crush mine, silencing any words, sucking them out of me, and a new heat spreads in my body. His kiss is punishment and it is possession. I cannot explain it better than that. It is a moment of clarity in which my anger seems to evaporate temporarily before it is back and I am kissing him—just as hard, with just as much fury.

My tongue lashes his and my hands are in his hair, rough, pulling at him, and I am kissing him as though I am still shouting at him with my touch.

He groans angrily and his body weight holds me to the wall, his strong legs straddling me, pinning me where I am. I think my brain is trying to tell me something, but I can hear nothing above the pounding of my heart and the rushing of my blood.

Desire is a whip, and it is lashing at my spine.

He drags his lips lower, nipping the skin of my shoulder with his teeth and teasing the racing pulse-point in my neck with his tongue. I groan, tilting my head back, knowing I need to stop this madness but accepting we are past that.

A line has been crossed. Not just crossed! Obliterated! There is newness to this. But I want to shape it, not be shaped *by* it. I need to be in charge—at least to some extent.

'Why do you care?' he asks, bringing his mouth back to mine and kissing me with enough force to hold my head hard against the wall. His hand drops to my dress, lifting the hem, and his fingers slide between my weak, shaking legs.

'Care...?' I mumble. What is he talking about?

He breaks the kiss but I have no space to think—not when his fingers are sliding inside me, his hand easily pushing aside the barrier of my flimsy underpants.

Oh, my God. I'm about to come. I swear, I'm this close. He swirls his finger around my wet muscles, teasing me, feeling me, and I am his. Completely.

'Why do you care who I fuck?'

The question is a gruff, deep demand.

I blink my eyes, trying to think straight. But he moves his thumb over my clit and I shiver, trembling in every bone of my body as I feel the wave building around me.

'I don't,' I snap through gritted teeth, sweat sheening my brow.

My eyes are shut, so I don't see him dip his head forward. It is a surprise when his mouth clamps over my breast, his teeth biting down on my nipple through the silky fabric of my dress.

My stomach lurches as he drags his teeth along my nipple, pulling, making me throb with pleasure. And his finger pushes deeper, then draws out. My own wetness glides across my clit as he thumbs my nerves, and I am lost. Exploded. Gone.

Heat shoots through me, bursting me apart, and I am panting loud and hard as he moves his head to the other breast.

Shit. It's too much. My muscles are clenching and my legs are hardly able to hold me up. I have had amazing sex, but something about this has blown all my experiences out of the water. Is it the illicitness of being with my boss?

My boss.

Jack Grant.

I groan in awareness of a moment I will undoubtedly regret, and then I groan at my weakness because I can't stop. There is a compulsion—no. An awakening. It is an acceptance of a truth I have fought too hard and for too long.

Two years of looks, laughs, infuriating arguments and differences of opinion have been leading to this. Two years of finding him in bed and fantasising about climbing in with him. I have resisted because he is my boss and I love my job—and because he's Jack-bloody-Grant. I have resisted acting on my deepest desires, but now I find it is impossible not to welcome his.

His hand drops to my side. His fingers dig into my flesh just enough to make me arch my back forward, but his hips rock me against the wall, crushing me with strength and passion. Hell, he's good at this. So, *so* good. So much better than I imagined.

And I've imagined a lot.

I whimper—a sound I don't think I've ever made in my life—as he brings his mouth back to mine, but the ghost of his kiss lingers on my breasts, making them painfully sensitised.

'Now do you think women complain after they leave me?' he asks, and he is stepping away, backwards, his eyes glinting in his handsome face as he stares at me with a confusing lack of passion.

There is colour in his cheeks and his chest is shifting hard, as is mine, with the pain of laboured breath. But his voice is steady and his eyes are cold.

His question doesn't make sense. I lift a finger to my breasts. They're tingling and swollen. I stare at him, unusually slow on the uptake.

'I give them what they want. What *you* want.'

And he turns sharply, stalking across the room and grabbing another drink. His back is to me as he throws back the glass and swallows, but I hardly register the movement. Shock is seeping into me. Shock at what we've just done.

Holy hell!

Was he proving a point? I am trembling, moistness slicks my underwear, my dress bears the marks of his kiss, my mind is tumbled—and he is *nothing*?

Feminine pique stirs in my gut. I fantasise about slipping the dress from my body and storming across the room. About pushing him to the floor and straddling him, making him admit he wants me.

I know he does. I felt the proof of his desire hard against my stomach. But sanity is returning, and with it the realisation that we have done something very, very stupid. There is no turning back. No unwinding time. I need to salvage my pride and get the hell out of his office before I do something really stupid. Like ask him to finish the job he started.

'I'll email you a full report on the server's feasibility tomorrow.' My words are pleasingly stiff.

He grunts. 'There she is. My cold-as-ice assistant.'

I straighten my back. I have *never* been his assistant and he knows it. He's goading me. Spoiling for another fight?

I narrow my eyes. 'Oh, I'm not cold,' I hear myself say. 'I'm very, *very* turned on.'

Perhaps my honesty surprises him. He turns his

face, angling it towards me without actually looking in my direction.

'If you'll excuse me, I'm going to go and…blow off some steam.'

I walk out of there calmly, even though I am awash with doubt. Let him make of that what he will. If he imagines me going to Wolf… So what? If he imagines me going home to masturbate, looking at a picture of him, then let him.

I don't know if I give a shit.

It is cold when I emerge from The Mansion, and drizzling with rain.

One of the decisions I made within six months of coming to work for Jack was to move to Hampstead, where he lives. The hours I work, I don't want to lose any more to a lengthy commute.

The Mansion is at the end of a long lane that comes out near the Heath, and just around the corner from a happy little school is my townhouse. A Dickensian brick with a shining red door and window boxes that have been sorely neglected over the summer. I should have planted them with pansies and strawberries, as they were when I first moved in, but I've never got around to it.

I shoulder the door inwards and slam it closed behind me with true relief.

But then I make the mistake of shutting my eyes and there he is. Jack Grant…head bent forward…mouth moving over my breast. I curse darkly—a string of angry words that would have knocked my mother sideways if she thought I even knew such language—and stride to the mirror in my entrance way.

My breasts are covered by two dark, wet marks. I

lift my fingers to them and trace their outline, shuddering at remembered sensations, desperate for more. More of him. More of this.

I groan loudly and stomp through to the kitchen.

What the hell just happened? He's my boss. My *boss*! And I know what he's like. I know how messed up he is. For two years I have kept all this swirling desire at bay. Why couldn't I control it tonight?

I pour myself a glass of wine in the hope that it will somehow reach back through time and wipe the experience not only from my memory but also from existence. It doesn't. Each sip reminds me of him, and the faint overtone of alcohol hits the back of my throat, making me crave him.

This is *not* good.

I walk more slowly through the house, up the narrow stairs—two flights. The house is tall and skinny, with one or two rooms on each of its five storeys. My office is on the first floor; my bedroom and bathroom are on the next. There are three bedrooms on the next few levels, and a roof terrace right at the top. I love it, but I am not here nearly enough.

I kick my shoes off, then flick the light on with the base of my wineglass, narrowly avoiding spilling Pinot Noir on the beige carpet. I pad over the carpet and strip off the dress as I go. I'll give it to charity as soon as I can.

In just my still-damp underpants, I climb into bed and pull the duvet up to my chin. Wineglass in hand, I stare at the wall.

It's not *that* bad, is it?

People must do this kind of thing all the time. We

work together. Hell, we practically live together. Something like this was kind of inevitable.

I cringe.

It's so *not* okay. Wasn't I just congratulating myself a few days ago on the Very Important Lessons I've learned from watching female bosses get derided and demoted over the years? Surely the cardinal sin for any woman in the workplace is to get involved with a colleague? And definitely not a senior, super-rich, super-yummy, fuck-around kind of colleague.

Ugh!

There are only a handful of us that work at The Mansion. Jack's two assistants, his driver, a bodyguard and me. We are all bound by a strict notion of confidentiality, and I think most of his staff are too afraid of me to get on my bad side anyway. So it's not gossip I fear.

It's Jack. And it's me. It's the respect I suspect I have sacrificed by letting this happen.

Letting it happen? My brain is outraged. My brain, after all, *did* try to stop it.

Sorry, I wasn't listening. I won't make that mistake again.

I pour the wine into my mouth, wincing at the astringent taste I really don't enjoy. I'm tired. It's been a long day and a weird night.

The last thing on my mind as I fall into a tortured, sensual sleep is a question about what tomorrow will bring.

He's at his desk when I arrive the next morning, coffee steaming in front of him, dark head bent. I move past, telling myself I would never do anything as cowardly as tiptoeing even as I hold my breath until I'm past his doorframe.

'Gemma? Get in here.'

Shit.

I squeeze my eyes shut, suck in a deep breath. I can do this. We just kissed.

You didn't 'just kiss'. He stuck his finger deep inside you and made you come.

Shut up, brain.

He sucked on your breasts and you fell apart at the seams.

Seriously, I'm going to lobotomise myself.

'Gemma?'

With a silent oath, I spin on my you-can-handle-anything Jimmy Choo heel and stride into his office with my very best appearance of calm.

'Oh, hi, Jack.'

Crap. He's wearing the pale blue shirt that makes his eyes look like bloody gemstones. It's unbuttoned at the neck and I can see a hint of dark hair curling above the top button.

'I didn't realise you were here.'

His smirk shows my lie for what it is.

'Sit.'

I arch my brow, staying exactly where I am, ignoring the wall to my left. The wall he pressed me against while he explored me intimately. My eyes stray to the bar instead. To the cocktail he was drinking last night.

'Sit,' he says again, and there is something in his voice that makes my nerves twitch.

There is promise in that command. Promise and heat.

'How are you?' The question, softly asked, makes everything inside me tremble.

'I'm fine,' I snap, to counteract that response. 'And busy. What do you need?'

His smile spreads slowly across his face. It is fire and it is flame and my brain is beginning to get very, very anxious.

'How did you sleep?'

Does he know I dreamed of him? That in my dreams he did very, very bad things to me?

I swallow, crossing my arms over my chest as the memories nip at my heels. They are in the room with us, swirling around him, me and the things we did. I can't give them more air.

'Did you want something?'

He stands up, and I am frozen to the spot as he moves confidently across the room, shutting the door and clicking the lock in place.

'I slept badly,' he says, ignoring my question, his voice sunshine on my cool flesh.

'Mmm…?' I murmur, making sure no warmth conveys itself to him. 'Maybe you should have tried a sedative?'

He strides to the chair across from his and holds it out. Shooting him a look laced with my fiercest resentment, I sit down, careful not to so much as brush against his fingertips. Fingers that have now been inside me—that have not just touched me, but have breached my barriers and found my throbbing heart.

Fingers that have undone me.

I am holding my breath again. Is that how I'm going to get over this little hurdle? Suffocate myself? Is that even possible? I'm pretty sure we have some breathing trigger in our brains, but my brain is a bit pissy with me so maybe it would conveniently forget about the button.

I push air out consciously, quietly, and he takes his seat.

'Anyway…' I prompt impatiently.

His smile is a flicker. Is he *laughing* at me? Arrogant arsehole! That'd be just like him. See? That's the problem! I *know* him. I'm not one of his other women. I know that he is as bastardy as he is sexy.

'How did you sleep?'

I blink at him, my eyes wide. 'You've already asked me that.'

'You didn't answer.'

I expel a sigh that speaks of anger. 'Like I always do. Seriously, Jack. My desk is covered in paper. I have to get to work.'

'*I'm* your work,' he says with a shrug.

Insolent bastard.

He leans forward, and while his face is casual there is an urgency in the flecks of gold that fill his eyes. 'Did you see him last night?'

I want to remind him of the salient fact I pointed out the night before. It's not his damned business. But I'm not sure I can say that with such conviction now that I've tasted his mouth; now that I've been stunned by his desire.

Can I skirt around his question?

'*You're* my work? Okay, the thing is I have the New York guys waiting on contracts, you have a meeting in a week that I have to prepare for and Athens wants your input—which means *my* input—on a lease agreement. And I need to—'

'Quiet.'

God! Don't hate me, but when he's bossy I *love* it. And he's almost always bossy.

I glare at him across his desk; it's best if he doesn't know that this is just about my favourite version of him.

'You're fucking telling *me* to be quiet?' I lean forward, and we're close now: almost touching. 'Seriously?'

'You're pissed off.'

'Damn right, I am.'

His laugh is soft. Throaty. Hot. 'Because we didn't finish?'

I flick my eyes shut. My cheeks are hot. 'What do you need?'

'Are you in a relationship with him?'

'Who?'

'Wolf DuChamp?'

I hide a smile. 'So you *do* know his name?'

'*Now* I do.'

His expression is unreadable. But deep inside me something stirs. *Hope.* Because isn't there an implication there that he knows about Wolf because of *me*? Because he wants to know about *my* life?

'So? What's the deal?' he asks.

'Are you jealous?' The words are a challenge; they escape unbidden.

His response is razor-sharp. 'Why would I be jealous?'

Crap. A stupid challenge, apparently.

'Forget it.' I scrape the chair back and stand, my eyes not inviting argument. 'Is that all?'

'You haven't answered me. How can it be *all*?'

I expel a breath angrily. 'I like him.' I shrug.

It's true. Not romantically, necessarily. But he's a nice guy. Good-looking. It doesn't matter that I've already ruled out a relationship.

'Are you fucking him?'

My expression is ice—even I can feel the chill that spreads through the office.

'Isn't this the question that got us into trouble last night?'

He stands up, slamming his palms against the desk, his eyes lashing me. 'Are you *fucking* him?'

It's loud. Not quite a roar, but close to it. I'm startled. This is outside the bounds of anything that's happened between us and we both know it. Then again, I guess we've obliterated boundaries now. They—like me—are in a state of flux. Changeability that is unpredictable and not good.

'Go to hell.'

I turn around and walk out of his office, but my knees are shaking and I feel really weird, as if I could cry—which, for your information, I haven't done in years. I *literally* don't cry. Not at sad movies. Not when my cat died.

But I'm shaking, and if he follows me I'll be really lost.

He doesn't.

I storm over to my desk. I wasn't lying or exaggerating. Piles of paper clutter every available inch of the thing. I turn my back on them and stare over the Heath, my eyes brooding.

This is a damned nightmare, isn't it?

My brain nods along smugly. *Told you so.*

CHAPTER THREE

IT HAS BEEN a week and I'm still here. What's more, my brain and I are almost friends again. I have been behaving. Working hard, speaking politely, keeping my sexy, kinky 'if only' thoughts hidden behind a mask of disinterest.

Of course it helps that I've hardly seen Jack.

He's been in Tokyo for four days, on a trip I would usually do with him.

Here's how it would go: Private jet. Limousine. Luxurious hotel accommodation—his apartment there is being remodelled. Meetings. Late-night debriefing.

You get the picture, and you no doubt see the risk.

'I have too much on,' I said when he'd decided he needed to go personally. 'Seriously, there's no way I can leave the office now.'

He ground his teeth together, looked at me as though I were pulling some soppy, emotional crap and then he nodded. 'Fine.'

He's due back today and my desk is no clearer—it's just a different heap of papers that covers it now. My phone bleats and I grab it up, my nerves not welcoming the intrusion.

Perhaps my impatience conveys itself in my brusque greeting.

'You sound like shit.'

The cackling voice brings an instant smile to my face. 'Hi, Grandma.'

'Where've you *been*, lovey?'

'Oh, you know…' I eye the paperwork dubiously. 'Living it up.'

'If only. Let me guess. You're at work?'

'You called my work number, so I suspect you know the answer to that.'

Another cackle. 'Are you coming to see me any time soon? I have something for you.'

'Another lecture on my priorities?'

'You're a smart girl. You know your priorities are out of order.' She sighs. 'Take it from a woman at the end of her journey. There's a big, beautiful world out there, and even if you devote your life entirely to travelling you'll still never get to see everywhere and everything.'

'God, that makes me feel both nauseated and claustrophobic. It's saccharine and overly sentimental even for *you*, Grandma.'

She laughs. I love her laugh. My grandma shines a light with her smile alone.

'Everyone's allowed a bit of sentimentalism at some point, aren't they? Especially at *my* age.'

'I travel *everywhere*,' I point out, flicking my calendar onto my screen and scanning it. 'In fact I'm off to Australia next week.'

Crap. With Jack.

'Oh, yes? That wouldn't be a work trip, would it?'

I grin. 'No. And by no, I mean yes—but I imagine I'll still get time to pet a koala.'

'You know they're not just crawling around the streets? You actually need to go bush to find one.'

I burst out laughing. '*"Go bush"?* Grandma, you're a Duchess. I think it's in the manual that you're not allowed to "go bush"—or go anywhere, really.'

I'm not joking. Grandma really *is* a Duchess. She married my grandpa, who was a decade her senior and had come back from the Second World War with what we'd now know as post-traumatic stress disorder. She was a nurse, and his family hired her to care for him—to "fix" him. She quit on the first day. There wasn't anything wrong with him, she declared. He was just different.

They got engaged that afternoon.

It's the only fairytale I believe in—and only because it has a macabre degree of reality to it. Grandma *did* fix him. He made her a princess—of the social variety—and she made him whole in a different way, just like she said.

We lost him years ago, and now *she's* the one who's a little bit broken. But still amazing. The most beautiful person in my life. My other constant.

Jack and Grandma. *Great.* An emotionally closed-off sexy widower that I should definitely know better than to want, and a champagne-swilling octogenarian, relic of the aristocracy. These two are the anchors in my life...

I shake my head, my smile rueful.

'Pish! I'll have you know I went bush and did a great many other things in my time.' She sighs heavily. 'And now it's *your* time—and you're spending it in some ghoulish house on the edge of the moors.'

'It's a mansion, actually, with state-of-the-art offices. And it's Hampstead Heath—not a moor.'

'Still...' A huff of impatience. 'You'll come this weekend?'

'I promise.'

I click in my calendar and make a note. Without entering my plans straight into my calendar I'm running blind. My eyes are dragged of their own accord to the entry for my parents' anniversary. *Ugh.*

'I suppose you got your invitation?'

'Mmm...' It's a noise of agreement that could mean a thousand things. 'Very elegant paper.'

I stifle a laugh. 'Stiff and unyielding.'

My implication hangs in the air, unspoken.

'Ah, well. At least there'll be booze.'

'And lots of it.'

I run a finger over my desk. Grandma and I got rather unceremoniously sloshed at the previous year's anniversary affair. If we hadn't been related by blood to the bride *du jour* we definitely wouldn't have been invited back.

'We'll do a rehearsal at the weekend,' she says, and I hear the wink in her words.

'Perfect. See you then.'

'Good, darling. Ta-ta.'

My phone rings again almost as soon as I hang up, and the smile is still playing on my lips as I lift the receiver and hook it beneath my ear. 'Yeah?'

'Gemma.'

His voice gushes through me like a tidal wave crashes over the shore. We've been in constant contact while he's been travelling—but only via email or text, and only in the most businesslike sense.

At no point has he reminded me of the way his mouth pushed me back, tasting me, robbing me of comprehension and hammering every last one of my senses. At no point have we discussed how he made me come against the wall of his office.

Hearing his voice now is as intimate and personal as if he strode into the room and straddled me, reached down and kissed me...

'I'm meeting some clients in the City. I need that presentation on the Tokyo project, as well as an up-to-date cost analysis and the report I had done. Meet me in an hour.'

It almost sounds like a question, but we both know it isn't. My body hums with vibrations. *I'm going to see him again.* It's the most alive I've felt in a week. My abdomen clenches in anticipation. Of what?

My body is getting carried away, but thankfully my brain is still lucid-ish. 'Fine,' I hear my brain say, cool and unconcerned. *Liar.*

There's a pause and I wonder what's coming next. 'Good.'

The little tick of approval sends a thrill along my spine. I hate that. I repress my pleasure.

'And, Gemma? Rose has something for you.'

I gather the documents he needs and quickly run through the project presentation, then step out of my office, laden with files and my MacBook Air.

Sophia and Rose are in the office they share, heads bent, and I smile crisply at them. 'I'm meeting Jack in the City. He says you have something for me?'

I address the question to Rose, who reaches into her

desk and pulls out an envelope. It has his dark, confident writing across the front. My name, scrawled in his handwriting. I resist the urge to run my fingertip over the letters.

'Thanks.' I nod crisply and Sophia reaches for her phone before I've said another word.

'Hughes—Miss Picton is travelling to the City.'

'Thanks.' I nod, pleased that things are working efficiently.

I hired Sophia to replace the last of Jack's assistants to quit. He's run through about six since losing Lucy; my own job has been filled a dozen times at least. I think it kind of bonds Sophia and me—a similar determination not to fail runs through us both.

'Will you be long? Shall I move your two o'clock?' asks Rose.

I can't reach my phone and can't remember off the top of my head what I have at two. I guess my blank stare conveys that, because Rose smiles at me kindly. How she's managed to work for Jack for three years is beyond me. She's a butter-wouldn't-melt kind of woman, and yet there's a quality to her that makes her oblivious to Jack's demanding requests and lack of charm.

'Carrie Johnson.'

'Right.' I nod distractedly, thinking only of the mysterious envelope. It's small and there's something inside.

Carrie is my friend who's looking for a new job—I have her in mind for something with the foundation, though I don't know exactly what yet. She was made redundant in the last round of restructuring at her com-

pany, and she's brilliant and incisive—far too clever
to let go.

'Yeah, shift it to tomorrow. Thanks. Please apologise for me.'

'Here.' Sophia scrapes her chair back and walks
towards me with outstretched arms. 'I'll help you to
the car.'

I hand over some of the papers gratefully. The offices are in a separate wing of The Mansion, and we
step out onto the short path that winds through a manicured garden before opening out into a gravelled court-
yard. It's really well designed to keep business away
from personal life—not that Jack has much of a personal life outside his fuck-fests.

At least, not that I know of.

I slide into the back of the limo, distracted; I don't
think I even acknowledge Hughes, which is unusual
because I like him and we usually have a nice banter
going.

You know everything there is to know about me.

I'm startled. The words come from nowhere and
I look over my shoulder, half expecting to see Jack's
cynical smile. Is that even true? Do I *really* know him
that well?

We've spent a heap of time together, that's true.
But I don't know if I would say I consider us well ac-
quainted. Out of nowhere the memory of his lips on
mine sears me, pressing me back into the leather seat
with a groan.

I reach for the envelope, and now I give in to temptation, running my finger over his scrawled writing
before tearing the top off.

My emotions are mixed as the object inside falls into my palm.

The distinctive dark red foil denoting a Cherry Ripe confectionery bar is instantly recognisable. I check the envelope for a note; there isn't one. But his meaning is clear.

I can't help it. I tear the paper off the bar and inhale.

Cherries will remind me of Jack forever. I don't think I can say I hate them anymore.

My gut clenches as I recall the intimate way his finger circled me, teasing every nerve ending, finding where to press to make me moan.

Fuck.

A shiver dances along my spine and it is still pulsing even as the car pulls into the underground car park of the City high-rise that houses Jack's offices. I gather he used to be based here a lot more. It was only after Lucy died that he set up shop, so to speak, at his home.

I make a point of smiling brightly at Hughes as I step out of the limo, laden with documents.

'Need a hand, ma'am?'

'I'm fine,' I demur.

I can't help but wonder if my cheeks are burning after the delicious thoughts that have travelled along with me.

Why did he stop? What happened to push him away from me?

I wanted everything. I wanted *him*. That technically makes me a complete idiot, right? Because I know he's a total man-whore, and I know it would make my job pretty untenable to be fucking Jack, but in that moment none of it had mattered.

Which only goes to show that I need to be even more on my guard with him.

I am *not* going to let this get out of hand. There are plenty of hot guys out there. Plenty of men who can kiss you like you're their dying breath.

Except I don't think that's necessarily true…

I've dated a fair few guys—most of them smart, handsome, powerful. I have a thing for that sort of man, I suppose. But none of them has done *this* to me. My mind is still mushy. I only have to close my eyes and remember the way it felt to have his body pressed hard to mine, almost holding me up with the weight of his strength, and I'm having palpitations and flushing to the roots of my hair.

The lift whooshes up and reminds me of the glass elevator in *Charlie and the Chocolate Factory*. It seems to be building up speed as we get nearer the top, and my tummy lurches as I imagine it bursting through the ceiling and flying into outer space.

It doesn't.

Is it wrong that I'm just a teeny bit disappointed? I always thought that looked to be so much fun—the way that elevator flew all over London's skyline.

The offices are buzzing, and it's so strange to be back in this kind of environment that I freeze for a moment, simply soaking in the noises. Anywhere else I've worked, it's been like this. I was like a headless chicken most days, surrounded by people who were every bit as harried and exhausted as I was. Exhaustion used to bleed into energy, so that I fed off a state of perpetual tiredness.

Someone rushes past, arms full of papers, and that reminds me that I need to do something with the files

I'm carrying. I begin moving quickly down the carpeted corridor, eyes straight ahead lest I be called upon to answer a query. The problem with being Jack's right-hand woman is that people see me as a substitute for him. I cannot visit this office without being waylaid with a dozen queries at least. Only I don't feel like talking to anyone at this point in time.

The conference room is at the end of the corridor. Two enormous timber doors provide entry to it. I shoulder my way in, making straight for the table, and I've just dropped the files down onto its glass top when I realise I'm not alone.

There's a movement to my right. No, a shadow more than a movement. But it captures my eye and I turn around slowly, careful to keep my expression neutral, because deep down I know who it is.

'You're here already,' I murmur, pleased with how unaffected I sound.

Especially when he's wearing his charcoal Armani suit with a crisp white shirt. And a dark grey tie. *Oh, God, help me.* I turn around, on the pretext of straightening the documents, but I feel the moment he starts to walk towards me and sweep my eyes shut.

My heart is pounding and my blood is gushing. What happened to pretending not to be affected by him? To keeping him at a distance?

'I'd say it's quicker to get here from City Airport than it is from my place.'

His voice is barely above a growl. It's primal and animalistic and a slick of heat runs through me.

'How was Tokyo?' I skirt around the table, laying information packs down as I go, checking each space has a glass of water.

He shrugs. 'Fine. And here?'

But his eyes are dropping. He's looking at my breasts as though he wants to take them into his mouth. As though he's remembering the way it felt to suck my nipple through the fabric of my shirt.

I moan, low and soft, so soft I don't think he catches it, but his lips flicker and I am in serious trouble. They are beautiful lips. Not full, but rather sculpted as if from stone. His face is peppered with stubble, as though he hasn't shaved the whole time he's been away.

I turn away, my breath uneven. I don't know what to do.

'As usual,' I say, no longer dispassionate, no longer smooth. My voice is jerky and unnatural.

I want to kiss him.

I *need* to kiss him.

I realise it in an instant and I turn around, back towards him. Our eyes meet and I feel a pulse of heat that I know I'm not imagining. It's a need so deep, so desperate, that I instantly imagine us fucking on the glass-topped conference table.

Is he thinking the same thing?

He takes a step towards me, his eyes latched to mine, his expression almost haunted. I part my lips on a breath and he stops just in front of me, catching that breath with his chest, and I can almost feel his lips on mine. It's a phantom kiss, but no less mesmerising than a real kiss because he's so close I can smell him...I can feel the warmth emanating from him.

'Did you get the chocolate bar?' he asks, and I feel my skin heat with memories.

I nod.

'Did you miss me?'

His voice is low and hoarse. I should laugh at him. That's what I would usually do. So why does his question fill me with a dawning despair? I can't ignore it. I'm suffocating under the realisation that I *have* missed him.

'Yeah, right,' I mutter, hoping it sounds more convincing to him than it does to me. 'I've been sitting in my office pining for you every day. One kiss and I've been writing your name in my notebook with little love hearts around it.'

I roll my eyes for good measure and so miss the moment he narrows his.

Jack isn't a man to be mocked. I know that, but honestly I wasn't intending to goad him. And yet I'm in no way surprised when his mouth crashes down on mine—for real this time, nothing phantom about it.

His hands pull through my hair, letting it out of the bun I looped it into earlier this morning. His fingers fist around it, holding my head under his so that his mouth has full access to me. And he *plunders* me. There's no other way to describe it. His mouth is a weight on mine and his tongue is angry.

Fierce heat pools between my legs.

He pulls on my hair as his mouth pushes mine, bending me backwards until my spine is on the conference table.

'Did you miss me?' It's a demand now, as he separates my legs and stands between them.

His cock is hard. I can feel it and unconsciously I writhe lower, trying to press myself against him, to connect myself to him.

His laugh is a dark imitation of the sound. 'Not now.'

It's a gruff warning, but insanity is cutting across me. I need him. If I don't have him I am going to scream. Sense is gone. Rational thought impossible. Even my brain seems to have momentarily forgotten itself.

I'm wearing a grey woollen dress and he rubs his hand over my breast, cupping it, holding me tight as his fingers graze my nipple. The fabric of the dress is coarse and the friction is unbearable.

His kiss is an insufficient prelude. I need so much more.

'More?' he murmurs, and I realise I must have spoken aloud.

He pushes my dress up my legs, and groans when he connects with the lace tops of my stockings. He digs a finger under one of my suspenders and then snaps it, hard, so that I make a sound of complaint. It's quickly muffled by a groan of pleasure as his fingers find my panties, pulling them roughly down my legs.

He stares at me and I wonder if I look as wanton as I feel. Hair tumbling around me like a golden halo, face pink, dress hitched up around my waist, legs spread around him.

His eyes are mocking as they meet mine. 'Haven't missed me, huh?'

I know I should say something sassy, pithy. Put him in his place. If his hard-on is anything to go by he's missed me, too. Or fantasised about me, at least.

'Like a hole in the head,' I murmur, but it's lacking spark.

He laughs, his hands firm around my calves as he spreads my legs wider, and before I can anticipate what he's going to do he brings his mouth down on me, running his tongue across my opening, lashing me with that same intensity he's just kissed me with. He pummels me, his tongue flicks my clit, and I am crumbling. I arch my back and stretch my arms over my head, my whole body trembling as wave after wave of need builds inside me. I'm so close to coming that I have to bite down on my lip to stop myself crying out.

'Have you missed me?'

He brings his mouth higher, dragging his tongue over my belly button, and his fingers push my dress up my body. His fingers find one of my nipples through the fabric of my lace bra and I jerk, because I am too sensitive already. I am only seconds from falling apart.

'Please…' I groan, moving my hips nearer to him, needing him to release me from this sensual torture.

'Please what?' he asks with a quiet anger I don't understand.

'Please,' I insist.

'Say it.'

Our eyes clash; it's a battle of the wills. I don't care enough to try to win it. At one time I would have fought tooth and nail, but not now. Now only one thing matters to me.

'Fuck me, Jack.'

'Here? In the boardroom at my office?'

I am going to hell. I don't even want to think about what my brain's going to have to say.

'Yes. Now. Please. Fuck me,' I whimper, so hot that I need him to *do* something. To fix this.

I drop my hand to my clit, but when I touch myself he grabs my wrist and pulls it away.

'No, that's cheating,' he whispers, his eyes on me as he loosens his belt and pushes his pants down just enough to release his gorgeous, glorious cock for me to see. I've seen it so many times, but now…? It's for *me.*

'Please…'

His eyes hold mine as he layers protection over his length, quickly, easily.

I push forward on the table, seeking him, and then he thrusts inside me, slamming me hard, and I feel the coiling of a pleasure that I cannot control. It is hot and fierce, and I cry out at the invasion that is so much better than my wildest fantasies.

His hands on my shoulders pull me up; he's so strong and I am lost in the moment. He pulls me against him and lifts me off the table so I can take him deeper, and I have a fleeting moment of gratitude for the heavy tint on the windows that surround the boardroom. His cock is spearing me, and I am wrapped around him, and he kisses me again—a kiss of such ownership and possession that I don't think I'll ever be able to lie to him again.

I *did* miss him.

'You want this?' he asks me, lifting my hips easily, gliding me up his length before pushing me down and making me cry out, my back arched, my nipples hard.

I nod.

'I didn't hear that.'

'I want this,' I groan, my fingers tearing through his hair, my mind completely scattered.

His laugh is throaty as he lifts me once more, but this time he eases me down to the floor, stroking up my dress as he goes.

I know outrage must show in my face, and I know he appreciates that.

'You want me.'

Mortification, anger and impatience are firing bullets across my desire.

I reach down and cup his hard-on, my eyes issuing him with a challenge. 'And you want me.'

He nods slowly, his eyes locked to mine. There is no mockery there now; instead I see something darker. Resentment.

'I want you.'

He turns away from me, pulling his pants up, buckling his belt, his shoulders set square.

He turns to face me, his expression suddenly businesslike. 'We'll talk after the meeting.'

I blink. The meeting. *Shit.* It's the reason I'm here but how quickly I've forgotten its existence.

My eyes fly to the clocks on the wall, each showing a different time zone. There are minutes to go before the others are expected, which means they could literally arrive *now*. I run my hands down my dress, then neaten my hair. No time to pin it back into a bun so I just smooth it with the palms of my hands until it sits neatly around my face.

I turn to face him, intending to ask for my underpants back. But the look he gives me is so fulminating that I lose my voice.

'You look like you've just been fucked,' he says darkly, and I sweep my eyes shut, shame spiralling through me.

What the hell has come over me?

I stalk towards him, my hand extended, waiting for the scrap of lace he must have somewhere, but he grabs my hand and jerks me against him once more.

'I like the way you taste.'

And he pushes me against the glass, and his hand pushes between my legs, and he pads a thumb over my clit. I'm already at breaking point. His body traps mine, but he doesn't kiss me. He watches me from a distance as he torments me with his thumb, moving faster until my breath is ragged and my eyes are huge.

'I want to taste you tonight. I want to spread your legs and dip my tongue inside you. Then I want to flip you over and take you from behind. You are so fucking hot when you're turned on.'

I whimper—a sound of pure confusion—because the pleasure of his words combined with the torment of his touch is almost more than I can bear.

I swear—a low, throbbing whisper—as my pleasure bursts like a waterfall. I come. I come hard. And as I do he slips a finger deep inside me, swirling it against my walls as my muscles contract. He stays there as I fall apart and then he glides his finger out and lifts it to his mouth, sucking on it while his eyes watch me.

The door is pushed inwards. It happens so quickly. I am still breathless, and I'm sure my orgasm is written all over my face. It's not like it was my first time, but this was *Jack*. He's Jack Grant—seriously sexy.

He should come with a health warning.

I hear my colleagues move into the room and I turn away on the pretext of getting myself a coffee from the back of the room.

He still has my underwear, and the tops of my legs are wet with the evidence of my own satisfaction. My breath is uneven.

God, this is going to be the longest hour of my life.

'Gem.'

Is that what everyone in the universe except me calls her? Her back has been towards me for at least three minutes and I've gone through the greetings and I'm waiting for her to turn around. I want to see her full red lips, her messy hair, her passion-soaked expression, and I want to know that I did that to her.

She angles her head sideways to greet Barry Moore, one of the transition team consultants on the Tokyo deal. 'Hey…'

Her smile is cool, her expression calm. The only sign that she was ravaged by me only minutes ago is that her nipples are straining against the fabric of her dress—something that might be explained by the ice-cold air conditioning.

'You did a great job on the summaries—thanks.'

'You got my email, then?' Her voice is calm and clipped, as always, those haughty, aristocratic syllables like plums in her mouth.

'On the flight over.' He nods, his eyes briefly dipping to her breasts so that I am flooded by an urgent need to bodily shove him aside.

'Jack? Shall we begin?'

I draw my attention away reluctantly, turning to the manager of the takeover team. 'Yes. Take a seat.'

I nod towards the table and find myself drawn to one seat in particular. I press my hands to the table-top, right where Gemma's legs were spread, and my eyes seek hers.

She meets them with fierce resentment.

She's pissed at me.

I just made her come in what I gather to have been a spectacular fashion and she's angry with me. Mind you, I guess I didn't really choose my time or place well. Leaving her breathless and wet right as some of the company's most senior staff filed into the room might explain her anger with me.

I sit down, my eyes not shying away from hers.

She chooses a seat at the other end of the table, on the opposite side. I cross an ankle over my knee and something catches my eye. Something dark and small. With a smile, I reach down and lift her underpants off the floor, palming them thoughtfully.

Her eyes are watching me and I see embarrassment creep along her cheeks, creating a hole in the armour of her professional composure. Her beautiful neck moves visibly as she swallows. And while I have her attention I lift my finger to my mouth and run it over my lower lip thoughtfully, tasting her openly.

Even from this distance I hear her sharp intake of breath and I smile.

I'm going to make her do that a *lot*.

CHAPTER FOUR

'I BELIEVE YOU have something of mine.'

Like my dignity. My self-control.

The meeting took almost two hours, and I managed to concentrate for the most part. But every now and again my insides would clench, reminding me that Jack had driven himself inside me—that he'd made me come against the glass windows of his boardroom and he hadn't experienced the same pleasure. I should have felt satisfied by that, but instead I was annoyed. Like he had proved how easily he could tear me apart and I hadn't done the same to him.

'Yeah…'

His smile makes my heart pound. Desire is slick in my blood, heavy and needy.

'So?' I put my hand out, then retract it, remembering belatedly that he has a habit of yanking me towards him when I give him the chance.

'So…' He reaches into his pocket and retrieves the underpants. 'I like the idea of you not wearing them.'

I roll my eyes. 'What a cliché. Do you expect me to dress a certain way for you from now on?'

His smile is a flicker at the corner of his lips. 'No…'

He wraps an arm around me easily, pulling me to

him. Of course he doesn't need my hand as an invitation. He has arms and hands of his own, and if he wants to touch me Jack Grant isn't going to wait for a bloody invitation.

'But if you did I'd enjoy doing what we just did over and over.'

I'm wet again. I can feel it building and I know that only fucking him—properly—is going to release this beast of need inside me. But I'm still fuming with Jack. How dare he do that to me right before an important meeting?

'No way,' I snap. 'Never again.'

He raises a brow, his smile genuinely amused. 'Really?'

And he reaches around for my hand, dragging it to his cock. I stare at him, challenging him, showing him I'm not afraid, as he curls my fingers around his length, rock hard inside his suit pants. My heart begins to bang into my ribs so hard that I absent-mindedly wonder if anyone has ever broken a bone that way.

'You *don't* want me to sprawl you out on the table and fuck you so hard you forget your own name?'

I want that so badly—but I have enough self-respect to know that he's playing with me. That the way he can knock me sideways is insulting.

And so I shrug. 'I think you've got a pretty fucking exaggerated idea of your abilities in bed.'

His laugh sends sparks of warnings through me. 'Really?'

'I'm not telling you anything you don't already know.'

I jerk away from him but my hand forms a fist; it wants to go back. To grab his cock and hold it tight.

'You want a demonstration of how wrong you are?'

'Arrogant son of a bitch…' I mutter, my eyes scanning the room until they land on my vintage Balenciaga bag.

I scoop it up, sending him a fulminating look. 'Keep them.'

I want him to chase me. To follow me and slam the door shut. To press me against it and moan into my mouth. To beg me to get on the floor and let him take me. Because at the smallest sign of conciliatory, normal behaviour I would do anything Jack asked of me.

But he doesn't.

I leave and I don't even know if he watches me go—I am too proud to turn around and check. My knees are shaking as I make my way through the corridor. It's only early afternoon, and I have a mountain of work to do, but suddenly I'm not in the mood.

I don't want to be near Jack.

Oh, really? my brain prompts sarcastically, rolling its eyes with such force that my head starts to throb. *Really?*

Really.

I jab my finger onto the lift's 'down' button and wait. As I step in I see Jack emerge from the boardroom, looking every bit the confident billionaire bachelor.

Ugh.

I press the button for the car park impatiently, and slam my palm against the 'door shut' button, holding my breath and praying I can avoid a shared lift ride with Jack to the basement. I'm not sure if I'd shout at him or jump him but neither is advisable.

I tell myself I'm glad when he doesn't arrive, jam his hand in the closing doors, out of breath from racing to catch me like men do in movies. The lift cruises downwards, taking my plummeting stomach with it.

Hughes is waiting in the limousine. I smile at him tersely as he steps out and opens the door for me, grateful to slide into the luxurious leather interior. I stare at the screen of my phone and that ridiculous sense that I might cry is back.

What the hell is happening to me?

I tap out a quick email to Sophia, asking her to clear the rest of my afternoon—from memory I had a phone conference scheduled and I'm really not in the mood. Nothing won't wait until tomorrow.

I double-check the itinerary I've been sent for the Australia trip—it's jam-packed, but that makes sense. Jack's too busy—and so am I, come to think of it—to go halfway around the world on holiday.

He's setting up an office in Sydney, which will start with a staff of almost four hundred to oversee two of the companies he's recently acquired there, as well as a winery in New Zealand that he's bidding on, should he be successful. It's a huge venture, and it's the first time I've been involved in anything like it.

Challenges like this are another reason I love working for Jack. Really, I was hardly qualified for this kind of job when I started working for him—my background in law and then banking give me excellent corporate insights, and yet this just works. He's always challenged me. Trusted me. Thrown down gauntlets and stood back to watch me pick them up.

He's doing it now, isn't he? Pushing me in ways I could never have imagined. But instead of meeting his challenge I'm acting like a terrified child.

A frown tugs at my lips. Why have I just run away from him? He wants to fuck me and I want that, too.

The car door opens abruptly and I tilt my head upwards, expecting to see Hughes's face. It's Jack instead, and he's visibly pissed off.

Ignoring the way my pulse immediately starts to fire in my veins, I send him a look of barbed curiosity. 'Yes? Can I help you?'

He doesn't answer. Instead he leans forward and taps on the glass that separates Hughes from us, then settles back into the seat beside me. The car glides out of its parking space, moving through the underground car park with finesse.

'Jack?' I snap, angling in my seat to face him fully.

'Not now.'

My eyebrows shoot upwards. Even for the dictatorial side of Jack, this is a tad too much. *'"Not now"?'*

'No.' He turns to face me, and there's such a searing… *something* in his expression that I blink several times, trying to understand him. This—us.

But I get *nada*.

'Okay, but I think we need to talk,' I respond after a moment.

He glares at me and my temper bubbles. 'I don't want to talk. I want to fuck.'

My jaw drops. 'You don't just get to *say* that!'

A muscle jerks in his cheek. He turns away from me, sits back in the seat, his body rigid, his face tight.

'Not another word.'

I'm not afraid of Jack. Not even a bit. Many times I've gone up against him, arguing my case until he either sees it my way or at least understands my perspective. I won't do that now. I'm too fond of Hughes, and the idea of subjecting him to the tirade I'm about to unleash doesn't appeal to me, so I bite my tongue—

literally—curling my fingernails into my palms as I stare out at the City.

It takes me a moment to realise we're not going towards Hampstead.

'I want to go home,' I say coldly.

His look is one of silent impatience, but before he can say anything the car pulls into yet another underground car park and comes to a stop right near the lift.

I can't describe how lost and confused I feel. I'm a swirling tempest of rage and insecurity, uncertainty and doubt. It's as though I'm in the middle of a swamp, reeds tangled around my ankles, water rising.

I want to fight with him. I'm angry. But I don't know what about! Putting into words what I feel seems impossible.

And then he speaks.

'Come with me.'

Three simple words, but they are enough because there is a plea in their depths.

I nod slowly, and there's a plea in that, too. *Please don't hurt me. Please don't use me.* I haven't even realised I feel it until this moment, but the idea of becoming to Jack what all those other women are is unpalatable. I weigh that against my need for him, and desire wins. I can only hope I won't regret it.

He pushes the button for the lift and then swipes a keycard. Soon the elevator is soaring towards the heavens—I'm in another lift, only this time with Jack Grant by my side.

'Am I allowed to talk now?'

He glares at me, then stares ahead until the lift doors open.

I guess not.

I stand with my hands on my hips, angrily admonishing him with my look. 'Nuh-uh. I'm not getting out until you tell me what's going on.'

'What's *going on*?' His tone shows incredulity.

He turns back into the elevator and lifts me easily, throwing me over his shoulder in a way I have only ever fantasised about. He carries me into an apartment—a palatial space. I gain a brief impression of glass, steel, white leather furniture and a state-of-the-art kitchen before he's storming down a tiled hallway and turning into a room.

A bedroom.

With an enormous bed in the centre and floor-to-ceiling windows that show a glinting view of London below.

'You are driving me crazy—that's what's going on. And I don't want to want you like this. I'm sick of waking up about to fucking explode because I've been dreaming about you. I'm sick of looking at you and imagining you naked every time we're in the same damned room.'

He drops me onto the bed but I'm too shocked by his angry confession to care. So he *does* feel it, too—this burning, all-consuming, unwanted, unwelcome, unasked-for need.

'So, if it's all the same to you, I want to fuck you properly—right out of my head—so we can go back to working together like damned adults instead of horny teenagers.'

My breath is burning my lungs, exploding out of me in fierce bursts. 'You think you can *fuck me out of your head*?'

'Yes.' He stares down at me, flicking his shirt open button by button.

My eyes follow his movement and though I've seen him naked before it was never like this. He's never been naked *for me*.

'Why? Why now?'

'Because I need you *now*.'

Still, my brain is shouting at me and, having ignored it in the past and had it lead me into disastrous temptation, I push up on my elbows and roll off the other side of the bed.

His eyes stay trained on me even as he continues to undress, and my throat is dry, parched. I feel like I've been dropped from a great height; I'm in free fall with nothing to grab. Gravity no longer exists.

'How *dare* you? You drag me here, to your…your… lair…' I spit angrily, only to have Jack burst out laughing.

'My *lair*?' He throws his head back.

He's so sexy. God, this isn't fair. I know what I should do. I know what I *need* to do. But he is laughing at me, and my pride is being thumped with each sound he makes.

I jump back onto the bed, storm across it quickly and step off the other side, surprising him with the force of my body against his, knocking him partway to the floor. He catches his balance, his hands steadying me even as I keep on pushing until we are at the wall.

'I'm not some nuisance you can get rid of. An itch you can scratch and lose.' I push a fingernail into his chest and glare up at him, my eyes firing at his.

'So what *are* you?' he demands roughly, his chest moving with each strained breath. 'Why are you all I can think of lately? Why do you consume my every damned waking thought? What sort of magic is this?'

I have needed to hear these words and they fill me

with something I don't understand. There is awe and confusion, and anger, too—because he is just like Mr Darcy, telling me he loves me against his will.

Only Jack's not promising love so much as sex, and Mr Darcy would *never* have made Elizabeth Bennet come pressed hard against a glass window on the forty-second floor of a high-rise in the City of London.

You know what else Lizzy wouldn't have done…?

I drop to my knees in front of him, and before he can guess what I want, or say anything to stop me, I move my mouth over his length, taking him deep—so deep that I feel him connect with the back of my throat.

'Holy hell, Gemma,' he groans, but he doesn't pull away.

His hands drop to my hair, tangling in its blond lengths. It is still wild around my face from when he almost fucked me in his office. His fingers pull at it and I glide my mouth over his shaft, rolling my tongue across its tip and tasting just enough of him to make my insides clench with fevered desire. I squeeze my fingers around his length and then take him deep inside my mouth again, my eyes travelling up his honed body to meet his. I see the swirling depths of emotion in them…I see that he is as lost as I am…and it is all that keeps me going.

If I'm going to feel like I have no clue who I am anymore then he should, too.

I move my mouth faster, rolling my tongue over his sensitive tip each time I am close to pulling away completely, and then his hands on my hair tighten, slowing me down, holding me still. His breath is rough, and I taste more of him spilling into my mouth.

I try to take him deeper but his fingers hold me still, the pressure on my scalp almost painful.

'This isn't going to end that quickly,' he says darkly, pulling me away completely and staring down at me before reaching beneath my arms and lifting me to stand. He stares into my eyes and there is so much triumph in my face that he must see it.

'Holy hell, Gemma,' he says again after a moment, and pulls me back towards the bed.

My heart twists achingly in my chest. He pushes me backwards, onto the middle of the mattress, and bends down, grabbing for something off the floor.

A second later I see what it is: his belt. He's naked—spectacularly so—and so hard and firm. He runs his hands over my arms, catching my wrists and pinning them over my head.

'Do you trust me?' he asks—deep, throaty, gravelled.

I shake my head but my lips are twitching. 'I trust you to make me come. I don't know if I trust you with anything else right now.'

His laugh is soft as he loops the belt in and out of the bedposts, and then grabs my wrists and incorporates them into it, pinning my arms behind me and above my head. It's not particularly comfortable.

'Then let me make you come again and again and again, Gemma.'

Gemma. The way he says my name like that—rich with passion and want—makes my body catch fire. Like it's not already an inferno!

He pushes at my dress, his hands on my thighs intimate. I still have no underwear on and he smiles to see my nakedness.

'You are beautiful,' he grunts, almost as though he's never noticed me before.

He brings his mouth down against me and I jerk my arms, wanting to touch him.

He laughs. 'And you're mine.'

Butterflies ravage me angrily. I *am* his. For this moment...for this night. Is this how it always is with him? When he makes love to those other women does it feel to them as though they are the only woman in the world?

The idea of being one of *them* is anathema to me.

'Remember what I told you in the boardroom?'

He pushes the dress higher, over my breasts, then leaves it bunched under my arms while he turns his attention to the scrap of lace that covers me. He doesn't bother to unclasp it—just lifts my breasts out of the delicate cups, bringing his mouth close to one of them and breathing warm air over the sensitive, erect nipple.

I arch my back instinctively and he laughs. 'Do you want this?' he murmurs, flicking it with his tongue, then circling the darker flesh slowly, teasing me, taunting me.

I nod, incoherent with need. 'I want *everything*,' I say seriously.

'Everything?'

'All of this,' I agree, pulling at my hands again, not caring that I am conceding all that I am to him. 'Please,' I add.

'Do you remember what I said?'

He is insistent. What *did* he say? 'Not to wear underpants again?'

He laughs, and then his teeth clamp down on my nipple and I cry out. The pleasure radiates through my body, slick in my abdomen.

'That, too.'

He rubs his stubble over my nipple and it's so sensitive from his mouth that I make a soft sound of surprise.

'I said I am going to fuck you until you can't remember your own name. Okay?'

I nod. I am lost, and I need him to see that. 'What's happening to us?'

His smile is haunted as he slides a condom over himself once more. 'What's happening? I think I've finally found my cure—that's what's happening.'

And he thrusts into me, so deep and hard and fast that the peculiar statement is lost. *I* am lost. I jerk my wrists so that the belt pulls against my skin, and I cry out in frustration that I can't touch him like I want to.

He is so big, and his dick reaches places inside me that I didn't know existed. He moves his mouth to my other breast and lashes his tongue against me as he pounds me hard. My hands jerk above my head. I am his prisoner, but even without the belt at my wrists I would be.

'Are you on the pill?' he demands, and I nod.

I am incoherent with pleasure, saying his name over and over again. My body is on fire. He is its master. His hands are rough on my smooth skin. He touches me everywhere as he moves inside me, thrusting deep, and still I want more.

'Please!' I cry out, not even sure what I'm begging for now.

But he knows what I need. Somehow he has mastered my body already, even though we are so new to one another. He pushes inside me and rolls his hips. I lift mine to meet him and I'm exploding, falling apart and flying at the same time, dropping through the earth's core as my body tries to cope with these sensations.

I groan loudly, wrapping my legs around his waist, holding him right where he is. But before the waves of my pleasure have begun to subside he guides my legs over his shoulders, so that I am bent over myself and he is so deep I see stars. Pleasure is tingling through me and he blows through it, rocking me in rhythm with his needs, kissing the sensitive flesh behind my knees before running his fingers lower to cup my arse.

I am shuddering with the strength of what he's doing to me. Then he pulls out, and I almost sob with the emptiness that threatens to cut me in half.

His laugh is dark. An acknowledgement that he understands.

His hands on my hips are strong; he flips me easily onto my stomach and my arms are crisscrossed, my dress tangled around my breasts and my neck.

I don't have time to tell him this, or to shift and adjust myself. He spreads my legs wide, puts an arm under my belly and lifts me higher. And then he drives into me from behind. He brushes against new nerves, makes me feel new things, and I gather from the muttered string of dark curses that fill the room that this is different for him, too.

His fingers dig into my hips as he holds me steady, thrusting into me and making me *different*, somehow. He drops forward, kissing my shoulder, dragging his mouth down my back before biting me on the arse— gently, but enough to make me groan. And then he's sucking the flesh at the small of my back, and I wonder if I'm going to have a mark there afterwards.

His finger between my arse cheeks surprises me. It is not somewhere I've been touched before, but it's only the lightest suggestion of a touch. A finger lightly pressing against my butt. A curious flash of wonder flies through me. But instinctively I shy away from it and he understands, laughing and moving his hand to my clit.

He strums me as though I am a guitar, and it's so intense that I almost cannot bear the pleasure. But I don't dare ask him to stop because perhaps he would and I couldn't bear that. It is like being prodded by a hot iron, though: I am burning up.

I explode angrily, loudly, my body shaking from head to toe, glistening with sweat.

He holds me tight, waiting for the waves to slow, to recede a little, and then runs his hands over my flat stomach to my neat breasts. He rolls my nipples between his finger and thumb, plucking them in time with his dick as he takes me again and again.

'It's not fair…' I moan, resting my head on the pillow, trying to catch my breath. 'I want *you* to feel this.'

He makes a noise. It could be agreement or amusement; I'm not sure. 'Do you think I'm not enjoying myself?'

No. I know he's having a good time. But that's not enough. I don't want to think I'm like all those other women, just being 'had' by him. I want to rock his goddamned world.

'Do I get to tie *you* up?' My words are as fevered as my sex-stormed soul.

He laughs and shakes his head, his chin gravelly against my back. 'No.'

'Why not? What's good for the goose isn't good for the gander?'

'Not in this case.'

'Isn't that a bit sexist?'

'You don't like it?'

My cheeks flame and I'm glad I'm facing away from him.

He brings the flat of his hand down on my arse, just lightly, but enough to spark the fire back into me, to make me forget what I want to do to him momentarily and enjoy what he's doing to me instead.

I push my arse higher and he massages me with his fingers, digging hard into the muscles there. I moan, low in my throat, and then he pushes inside me. I'm so wet. I drop my head lower and now he reaches up, unclipping the belt and freeing my wrists.

He pulls out of me. 'Turn around.'

A command. I obey, even though a part of me wants to tell him to stuff it purely as a point of pride.

Flat on my back, I stare up at him, my breath rushed, my lower lip sucked between my teeth.

'I want you to see what you do to me.' The admission is hoarse; as though drawn from deep in his throat.

He pushes my legs up again, lifting them over his shoulders as he drops into me, and I welcome him as though he's been absent for months, not moments. He laces his fingers through mine, pinning my arms either side of me, and he stares down at me as he takes me once more.

I sweep my eyes closed as another wave begins to build, but he drops his mouth to mine and pulls my lower lip between his teeth, pressing into it just enough to startle me into looking at him.

'I want to see you. And I want *you* to see me.'

Mesmerised, I can't look away. I watch as his face contorts with pleasure and he rocks inside me, and my own pleasure rides high with his until we are climaxing together, my body flaming to his, leaping with his, burning like his. It is him and me, and no one else in the world exists or matters.

He explodes inside me—a powerful release that makes him cry out loudly…a guttural sound that rips through the room. And I echo it deep within my soul. I am as overwhelmed as he.

He stays above me, his breath uneven, his eyes almost accusing as my own climax recedes, and I am left weak and confused by what the hell just happened to us.

I stare up at my boss, at the man who's just given me—I don't know…four orgasms? Five orgasms? I've lost count. It's still the afternoon and my body is covered in goose bumps.

Holy shit. Is this what it's like with his other women?

They are like ghosts, immediately hovering on my subconscious. I hate it that they're there, but my brain clearly needs me to remember them. To remember what Jack's like.

'So I suppose you don't get complaints after all,' I murmur, running my fingertips down his back. Like mine, it is wet with perspiration.

'Not so much.'

He pushes up, with a smile on his face that somehow doesn't fill his eyes. He presses a light kiss to my forehead and then stands.

'I'll get Hughes to take you home.'

The words seem to be spoken in a foreign language for all the sense they make to me. He'll get Hughes to take me home? Is he fucking *serious*? Am I being *dismissed*?

I smile, even as my mind is reeling from the sheer rudeness of that statement. 'I need to finish something at the office.'

I am amazed by myself. How do I sound so unbothered? So casual? It's a bald-faced lie, but it's the best I can come up with while my body is numbed by shock and fulfilled desire.

He nods. 'Fine. He can take you there.' Another tight smile. 'You're okay to let yourself out? I'm going to grab a shower.'

Jesus fucking Christ. *Is* he indeed?

'I think I can find a door without a map,' I drawl sarcastically, reaching for my phone without so much as a smile.

I flick it to life and load my emails, but the words swim before me like one big puddle of grey matter.

Which is what his brain is going to be against the crisp white wall if I don't get the hell out of there.

He walks towards a door across the room and I continue staring at my phone. Yet I know he's paused and is watching me. So I smile at an imagined joke on my phone, then pretend I'm typing a reply.

If you'd asked me an hour ago what could go wrong I would have said exactly this. Pushing past the boundaries we've always wisely obeyed, only to have Jack reinstating them just as fast as he's able—brick by brick, blocking me out.

My fingers move over my phone but I'm play-acting, doing what I can to distract him from the fissures running through my heart, my hopes and my confidence.

Eventually Jack moves into the bathroom and I hear the shower running.

Arsehole.

It might have been the best sex I've ever had, but I'm pretty sure it was also the biggest mistake of my life.

CHAPTER FIVE

'AMBER.' I SMILE, meeting the redhead's eyes with genuine interest.

Lucy's sister is ten years older than Lucy was, and she has the same pale skin and dainty features—at least going from the photographs I've seen. Her eyes are enormous and brown, her smile slow but genuine. She is naturally plump and attractive.

I like her instantly.

'The angelic Gemma,' she responds, her Scottish accent thick. 'I've been looking forward to meeting the woman who's tamed my brother-in-law.'

Tamed him? Not bloody likely.

Flashbacks of the previous afternoon flood my brain and I push them away. I cannot think about how it felt to be made love to by Jack Grant. No—*fucked* by him. Fucked hard. So hard, so hot… Oh, my God. My insides clench with remembered need. It's a visceral awareness, and actual biological need throbs through me on a cellular level. It's every bit as compelling and real as thirst, starvation and fear. It is a need strong enough to fell me at the knees.

I swallow, hoping to calm my raging, insatiable desire. 'I'm pretty sure he's untameable,' I say, with only a hint of desperation, gesturing that she should take a seat.

I've moved us to the small conference room on-site at The Mansion. Thankfully it's nothing like the office in the City, with its modern decor and imposing outlook. This is a room far more fitted to an ancient home on the edge of Hampstead. Still expensive, with luxurious leather recliners, but homely, somehow.

'Put up with him, then. You must have the patience of a saint.'

'I must,' I agree.

'Gemma is actually very impatient.'

His voice enters the room before he does, and I straighten in the chair.

'If I don't give her what she wants straightaway she begs me until I give in.'

My cheeks flame and I'm grateful that Amber is standing and moving across the room towards Jack—arsehole that he is. How *dare* he say something so bloody obvious? I know we're both thinking of how I begged him to make love to me the day before.

My eyes cling to Jack and Amber, morbidly fascinated, as they embrace. It's a hug of true affection and, yes, grief is there, too. He's wearing navy blue pants and a pale blue shirt which he's rolled up to just below the elbows. It's a linen material, and it's crinkled a little around the chest, showing he's been sitting in it for quite some time.

He keeps an arm around Amber's waist as they walk deeper into the room. She takes an armchair opposite me and he sits beside her, facing me, aligning himself with her.

They are family. I'm the outsider.

It hurts. Possibly even more than the showering-straight-after-sex thing.

Did he need to drink copious measures of Scotch to forget me last night?

My eyes drift to his face to find him watching me. Intensely watchful, I would have to say, peeling away my skin and analysing each beat of my heart.

I blink, careful not to react, and then turn back to Amber. 'How's everything going with the launch preparation?'

'Aye, good. We're getting there. I've staffed the main headquarters and we're just getting the international charitable recognition worked out to allow foreign donations.'

'Advertising?' Jack chimes in.

'We're meeting with two agencies next week to select a final campaign. It's looking like it will be print and digital-heavy, with the possibility of sponsoring a major sporting event over the summer—possibly the cricket.'

Jack pulls a face. 'Bloody hell. The *cricket*?'

'Oh, come *on*. Lucy would have wanted it.' Amber grins, pushing a finger into his shoulder in a further sign of their casual camaraderie.

It's strange that I don't often think of Jack like this—as a member of other spheres.

Here, it is him and me and the work we do together. It consumes so much of my life that I must admit I'm surprised to realise he has other people, things, memories and hobbies. Jokes and history.

Did Lucy watch cricket while Jack groaned about it? Did they laugh about his aversion to any sport other than rugby?

I blank the thoughts—or try to. But they're gnawing at my mind, unfolding like a concertinaing piano accordion that's ever so slightly out of key.

'It'll be a good show,' Amber says loudly, her smile encouraging as she winks in my direction.

Despite the fact that she's forced me to walk through a door that shows me the ghosts of Jack's Happy Past, I like her immensely, and the more she speaks about the foundation the more I know we've absolutely made the right decision. She's intimately informed on all the matters I need to consult with her about. She's thorough and quick and funny. And she's uniquely motivated to make the fundraiser a success.

She's Lucy's sister, and Lucy is dead, but I am jealous of Amber suddenly. It's ridiculous. An emotion entirely unworthy. But watching her talk, with her big red lips and her animated face, I feel wan and boring in comparison.

I would have been bland compared to Lucy, too.

I look downwards as Amber launches into a description of the view from her office. I'm wearing one of my favourite dresses—a shift in olive-green with bell sleeves and a boat neck. Oh, but it's so conservative and drab! Just the kind of dress my mother would adore. I chose it for the length of the sleeves, which fall to partway down my hands, because my wrists—which I see I've now accidentally left uncovered—have a dark band of bruising around them.

Belt-burn. *Thanks, arsehole.*

I nod at something Amber's said, my eyes moving of their own accord to Jack's face.

He's looking at my wrists, too, and the colour has drained from his face. I shift self-consciously, uncrossing and crossing my legs and drawing my sleeves lower in the process.

'Amber, we can discuss the rest over lunch. I know Gemma's got a desk full of crap to deal with.'

'*Your* crap!' Amber laughs good-naturedly, totally relaxed.

'That's her job,' he says pointedly.

Amber rolls her eyes. 'How you put up with him is beyond me.'

But she stands, straightening the crinkles out of the front of her skirt as she moves towards me. I hold out a hand to shake but she ignores it and pulls me into a hug instead.

'We've spoken so many times I feel like I already know you. But it's been lovely to finally meet you.'

'Likewise,' I murmur, stepping away from her with cringe-inducing coldness. Something else my mother would approve of! Standoffishness is a bland green dress. *Great*. I'm everything I swore I'd never be.

'Gemma? I need a moment with you, please.' He turns to Amber. 'Why don't you wait for me in the car? This won't take long.'

'I have a few calls to make,' she says, and nods, clipping out of the room.

He walks behind her, but only so far as the door, which he pushes shut emphatically and slips the lock across with equal force. And then he is prowling towards me. Yes, *prowling*. That's absolutely the word.

I have about four seconds to pull myself together. Four seconds to ignore the hammering of my heart and the throbbing of my libido. Four seconds to remind myself that he's my boss, and a total ass to boot. To remember how I felt when he rolled off me and all but asked me to leave his bed not two minutes after deserting my body.

No one has the right to make me feel like that. *No one*. And certainly not twice.

'That went well,' I say efficiently, leaving no room for the personal. 'I'm thrilled she's going to be at the helm of the foundation.'

A muscle jerks in his cheek—as though he's grinding his teeth or something. He catches my wrists and lifts them, pushing my sleeves up my arms to reveal the full extent of my bruising. He closes his eyes as he runs his finger over them, as though fortifying himself to look properly.

'You're hurt.'

I swallow, not liking this side of him any more than I do the bastard side that showered as soon as he'd pulled out of me. This is scarier, because it's doing really odd things to my heart and my tummy, seeing him show this kind of humanity and compassion.

I jerk my wrists away. 'Yeah… Can't you tell? I'm in agony.' I roll my eyes for good measure. 'It's just a couple of bruises.'

He nods, but there's a look in his face that I don't know if I ever want to see again. 'Listen, Gemma…' The way he says it rolls my stomach. 'About yesterday…'

'It's fine.' My smile is a flicker across my face and then it's gone. 'I *know* you.'

He shakes his head. 'No, you don't understand.' His frown is one of frustration. 'Let me explain.'

I swallow. *Be strong. Remember Shower Gate.* 'You don't need to explain,' I say firmly.

Please don't let him explain. Without an explanation there's ambivalence. But if I have to listen to his regrets, worse, his apology…?

'It was good. I had fun. Let's leave it at that.'

I walk towards the door, needing an escape. My legs are unsteady and my throat is parched and sore—like it's been flamed with a blowtorch. I walk away from him because my sanity depends on distance.

But this time he follows. He puts a hand on either side of me as I reach the darkly panelled door, so that I'm trapped by him. I freeze, staring straight ahead while my body goes into overdrive, his nearness impossible to ignore.

'You want to leave it at that?' he asks, his hand dropping to my hip.

I close my eyes, waiting for the hammering of my pulse to slow. As if it's going to.

'You want to forget what that felt like? Never do it again?' His fingers run lower, down my leg to the hem of my dress. 'Say the word and I'll step backwards. I'll stop touching you. For good.'

I nod, but 'the word' clogs my throat.

'Spread your legs apart.'

You do that and I am outta here. Love from your brain.

'Jack…' I say, his name thick and hoarse.

'I've been wondering all morning,' he says quietly. 'Did you listen to me?'

And his hand creeps under my dress, up my leg towards my bottom, where he finds the fabric of my knickers and flicks at it, hard enough to make me jerk.

'No, you didn't. Shame… Because if you weren't wearing underwear I could take you right now. Here against the door. Would you like that, Gemma?'

I groan, completely frozen by the imagery of his words.

'I'm going to fuck you now unless you tell me not to.'

Not only can I not find the words, I nod my head in total surrender. I hear his exhalation of breath and smile weakly. I move to turn around, but he keeps his hands on my hip—firm.

'No. Like this.' And he pulls me backwards, bending me at a ninety-degree angle.

He doesn't remove my underpants. He links both hands around them and pulls until they tear, dropping them to the ground.

I stare at them with surprise and impatience. 'They were really expensive,' I say darkly.

'They were in my way.'

I hear him unzip his trousers, then the familiar sound of foil being torn, rubber being snapped onto his length, and then he's inside me. No preamble, but— let's face it—the whole morning's been a total exercise in tantric delay. He runs his hands over my back as he thrusts into me and I splay my fingers wide against the door, my body taking his possession as though it's what I need to stay alive.

I am hot and cold all over, and about to come when he pulls out. It is so like the torment of the day before— the utter outrageous shock of desolation—that I cry out hoarsely into the room.

'You'd better not fucking stop,' I say angrily.

He straightens me and turns me around, pushing me hard against the door and kissing me until my knees are about to give way.

'Think of that as an IOU.' He pulls away, his eyes

meshing with mine. 'One I intend to collect.' He scoops down and grabs my underwear, dangling the scrap of fabric by one finger. 'And no more of this.'

I gape at him. 'Is that an order, *sir*?'

'You'd better damned well believe it.'

'Okay, I'll call HR and have it added to my contract.'

He kisses me again and my body sways towards his; I give up the sass immediately.

'Fuck me more,' I say into his mouth.

'Wild horses won't stop me.' It's a growl. 'Later.'

Five minutes later, I'm staring at my desk, a frown on my face.

What just happened?

It's like some kind of cyclone came into the room and settled down on top of us. All that's needed is for us to be close to one another and *bam!* The world loses its usual governance and we are wild, unshackled animals.

I tilt my head forward, catching it in my hands.

I've never felt like this.

I've always been able to control the men in my life, and I've always, *always* known what I want from them. Relationship decisions have, historically, been made by the same part of my brain that runs my career and all other aspects of my life.

I know some people talk about 'love at first sight', but that's always been a good clue to me that those people are batshit crazy.

Oh, I'm not saying I think I'm in love with Jack! I'm sexually tormented, not a sadist, and loving Jack would be stupid. But I don't have any brainpower or willpower around him.

He has all the power. *Sex* power. It makes me uneasy to acknowledge that and to accept that I would walk headfirst into whatever it is we're doing just to be with him some more. He's that good.

My body is a livewire, arcing through space, waiting to be grounded by him. But he doesn't ground me—he flares me into a violent electrical storm.

I drive him crazy, too. I remember, in a drowning attempt to have faith in my own abilities, that when I went down on him he was mine. Completely.

I don't think Jack welcomes this development any more than I do. I think his brain is probably giving him as hard a time as my own... What we had before *worked*. Sure, I pretty much had to pull up my big girl pants in the form of Maid Marian's chastity belt to make sure I didn't give in to the sexy man-pull of Jack Grant. But professionally we're a great team.

And losing that is far riskier for him. I'll get another job when I want one—I'm forever being headhunted, in fact.

My frown deepens as I open my second drawer and rifle through it, my fingers curling around the card of the most persistent caller. Andrew Long from Saatchi & Long. He's offered me some seriously awesome job opportunities in the last year, and every time I demur he tells me I must be on an incredible package.

Little does he know! I *am* very well-paid; Jack knows he can't afford to lose me. But, more than that, I get to stare at Jack-fucking-Grant all day.

Oh, God.

This is hopeless. I scrape my chair back, dropping Andrew's card back into the drawer and pushing it closed, scooping my bag up and pulling the strap over my shoulder.

'I'm going out,' I call as I pass Sophia and Rose. 'Back soon.'

Sophia waves in acknowledgement. I keep walking, my bare ass making me feel both turned on and self-conscious as I step out into the weather. It's cold, but I forgot my coat and I don't really care.

'Ma'am?' Hughes straightens from where he's been leaning beside the limo.

'Do you just lounge about out here all day, waiting for me to walk past?' I ask teasingly. I know how busy he is.

'Better than watching paint dry. You can actually *walk* in those things?'

He nods down at my Louboutins with a smile on his lips. They're two-inch spike heels and, yes, I'm very, very good in heels.

'I could run a marathon in them,' I say, and wink. My hair is in a ponytail today and the wind blows past, flicking it against my cheek.

'Well, save yourself the effort today.' He reaches for the door handle. 'Where to?'

I look at him blankly. It's a fair question; one to which I have no answer. 'I'm just going to go for a walk,' I explain. 'I need a coffee.'

'A coffee?' His look is one of sardonic amusement. 'You mean that spaceship's stopped working?'

I shake my head. The high-end pod machine Jack's had installed makes great coffee and we both know it. 'Okay, you caught me. I want a *pain au chocolat*.'

'Really?' He grins, arching a brow. 'A weakness for patisserie goods…interesting.'

I shrug. 'Certain days,' I say in explanation.

'Say no more.'

'See you soon,' I say in farewell. Then, as an afterthought, 'Need anything?'

'No, ma'am.'

So, I've banged her against a door in the conference room of my home office *and* against a window of my boardroom in the City. And while my sister-in-law was waiting in the car for me, too.

Jesus.

The Gemma Conundrum is getting out of hand. I woke up this morning knowing I had to apologise for yesterday, to tell her I'd regretted having sex with her the second we were done. That it had been a colossal, asshole mistake.

And then she walked away from me and I panicked.

Apparently Gemma only listens when I'm inside her.

So? What? I'm going to have sex with her any time we disagree? Any time she gets annoyed?

Amber laughs at something and I smile, but my mind is on Gemma and the promise I made her—that I'd collect on my IOU later today. The thought of not doing so makes some part of me want to shrivel up. So I accept the inevitable. We're going to fuck again.

My cock tightens instantly, straining against the fabric of my pants. Is she still naked beneath her dress, waiting for me? Wanting me?

I sip my wine, and say something in response to Amber's question—I'm amazed that any part of my brain is ticking on as normal, absorbing what's being said and answering in kind, even while most of me is absorbed by the question of my assistant.

I *love* sex. I love it because it lets me forget about Lucy and what I no longer have. But Gemma is different—because I can't just fuck her and walk away for good. I have to see her every morning—and what if she starts to want more from me than I can possibly give?

'Hey, Grandma.' I can't help but smile as she answers the phone in her sunny little room.

I hear her sip her tea and imagine her lips smiling against the bone china rim. 'What's up, lovey?'

'Nothing's up. How are you?'

'It's the middle of the day on Friday and you're calling me. What's up?'

I shake my head, but those damned tears that have been dogging me for days are threatening to fall. I blink my eyes angrily, staring at a family as they walk past me. Mum and Dad holding hands and three small children of varying degrees of growth and rugged-upness run past, looking as though they're being pulled back by a magnetic force when all they want is to sprint along.

'And is that birdsong in the background?'

I bite into the *pain au chocolat*; crumbs flake down my front. Absent-mindedly I brush them aside. 'I'm on the Heath.'

'You mean you've unshackled yourself from that desk?'

I laugh. 'Yes, Grandma. From time to time I *do* get out.'

'Have you spoken to your mother recently?'

I furrow my brow. Grandma is the only person on earth who understands my relationship with my parents. She understands that I love them, but in a dutiful way—they did give me life, after all. They also gave me self-doubt and insecurity and a sense that I'd never be good enough for anything other than the life they envisaged for me. Grandma tunnelled me right out of that existence, though.

'Not for a week or so.' Actually, it's closer to a month. 'You?'

'They called yesterday. They're in Cambodia.'

I arch a brow, imagining my perfectly manicured, elegant mother in Cambodia, of all places. 'I trust the Shangri-La's penthouse is sufficient?'

Grandma laughs. 'Well, you know—they're doing volunteer work.'

I burst out laughing at this ongoing joke between us. My parents are incredibly wealthy, incredibly entitled aristocrats and they have apparently reached a point in their life where they're bored with that and are looking to 'make the world a better place'. So far this has involved paying a lot of money to buy shoes for children in Africa, travelling to Lithuania to learn about child smuggling and now a trip of Southern Asia to 'help provide vaccinations' to the poor.

I wonder how helpful my mother—who faints at the sight of blood—and my dad—who can't stand heat, mosquitos or poverty—are actually capable of being.

'I think they're going to cut their trip short,' Grandma says, almost managing to keep the droll amusement out of her voice.

'Oh, I'm *so* surprised by that.' I fail miserably. 'I daresay the philanthropic community of Cambodia will breathe a sigh of relief when they board their flight home.'

'Yes, well… Their hearts are in the right places,' she murmurs, and I nod.

Perhaps.

'They'd do better to donate to a foundation,' I say. 'Money is what these people need. And then trained staff can do their jobs without westerners assuaging their guilt over the quality of our lives getting in the way.'

'Phew, that's been building up for a while, has it?'

'Sorry. I just can't stand volunteer tourism. If I see one more photo of a schoolfriend posing with emaciated children in Africa I'm going to punch something.'

'Darling, it all brings attention to good causes.'

'Yeah—and it makes rich people feel better about their rarefied existence in the process.'

'Mmm…'

Grandma is nodding. I just know it.

'So nothing's going on, then?' she asks.

The children on the Heath are running now, and the mother and father are watching, holding hands, laughing as the littlest one tumbles down and lands in the middle of some wet grass. One of the older siblings scoops him up, cradling him and spinning in circles until the little one's laughter peals across the grass towards me, hitting me like a slap in the face.

I'm not clucky. I don't want children. The agony of my own childhood is one I would never inflict on another. Oh, it's not like I was abused or anything. My parents loved me. Loved me enough to hire only the best nannies and tutors and horse-riding coaches. To send me to the very best schools… Clue: the best schools for meeting handsome, eligible husbands-to-be.

And they loved me enough to question my sanity when I enrolled in joint honours at Oxford and then post-grad at the LSE. But there was Grandma in the front row when I accepted my Master's degree.

'I'm just flat out,' I say quietly. 'Work's crazy at the moment.'

Grandma is quiet, taking this in. Then, 'You're coming for lunch tomorrow?'

Tomorrow? *Shit*. It's almost the weekend. But the idea of seeing Grandma makes my heart soar. 'Lunch? Yeah, sure.'

'And you'll bust me out of this hellhole again? Take me out for so much champagne I get woozy and disgraceful?'

I laugh, because the 'hellhole' nursing home Grandma is in costs more per year than most people earn in a lifetime and is the last word in luxury. She has a *personal butler*, for crying out loud. But the staff there don't entirely approve of her love of bubbles, whereas I am more than happy to serve as her occasional enabler.

'Yep. You betcha.'

I stand up, giving one last look at the family as they move over the crest of a hill and disappear out of sight, then I walk across the grass, making my way to the gate nearest the lane that leads to Jack's mansion.

I try not to think about whether Jack will be in the office when I get back.

CHAPTER SIX

IT'S JUST AS well I'm busy. Between running one last glance over the Wyndham contracts, checking the files I'll need and locking down the details for Australia, responding to some urgent emails and looking at some high-level staff CVs for the foundation, the day passes quickly.

It is evening before I know it and I am still at my desk. My phone bleeps just as I'm packing up.

I'm in the City. Hughes will bring you here when you're done.

I read the text three times, my bemusement growing with each moment. True, I'd basically begged him to fuck me earlier that day, but this is hardly a masterpiece in flirtation and seduction.

Do you need me for something?

I fire the message back, lifting my bag over my shoulder and switching the lights off at the door.

You know what I need you for.

I don't reply. I don't know why. But I make my way outside and smile at Hughes—possibly the only guy in the company who works hours as long as Jack and mine. He doesn't have a family. He was in the army and returned from three tours of Iraq ready for a change. He's smart, safe and we trust him implicitly.

We.

I do that a lot, but I don't mean 'we' in a romantic sense. It's just that we've almost become partners over the years without either of us realising it.

'I'm meeting Jack at his place in the City,' I murmur.

When I was sixteen my dad caught Roger Cranston and me fooling around in the kitchen. I was so mortified with embarrassment that I spent the next week making up elaborate stories that would explain exactly why Roger had been kneeling in front of me, my skirt pushed up my legs.

He dropped a pen and...um...I was reaching for another...

I feel that now. That same sense of embarrassment— like I've been caught doing completely the wrong thing and need to explain. To *Hughes*, of all people.

My cheeks flush pink and I don't meet his eye. 'I need some documents signed.'

He pulls the door open and smiles. 'Long day?'

'Yeah, you could say that.' I sit down, careful not to flash my naked self to him, then sink back into the leather seat.

I read the news on my phone as we drive, catching up on what I've missed while I've had my head down the Jack Grant wormhole all day, and discover that a police manhunt has ended with the suspect being shot, and that a chain of supermarkets is at risk of bankruptcy.

We're at his apartment block quickly, though, and the door opens to the familiar bank of lifts. Hughes presses a button, then swipes a keycard so that I'm granted access to the floor Jack's penthouse is on.

'Thanks. Goodnight, Hughes.'

'Goodnight, ma'am.'

I laugh. 'You know I hate it when you call me that.'

The doors swish closed on his wink.

I'm still smiling when the lift opens—but it's transformed into a frown of curiosity as I step into Jack's place. A couple of lights are on, casting an ambient glow, but otherwise it's dark. There are lights coming from beyond the glass and, curious, I walk towards it.

'Hey.'

Jack's voice comes from down the hallway and I turn to see him emerging from one of the rooms, a towel knotted loosely around his waist.

'I didn't know you were on your way.'

My eyes have dropped to his bare chest. To its rhythmic rise and fall as he breathes, to the smooth tan that covers him and the hint of ink I can see above the towel.

I swallow, my throat dry, and force myself to meet his eyes. 'How was your day?' Crisp, professional. Safe, good.

'Fine.'

He unwraps the towel, uncaring of his spectacular nudity, and brings it to his hair, towelling it dry. He's semi-hard, and God knows I want to jump him then and there.

But I don't. I'm not sure why, but something holds me immobile.

'Good meeting with Amber?'

'Yeah. You were right about her. She's a good pick for the job.'

'I think she's got the perfect combination of experience and passion.'

His nod is droll. 'She sure has, Miss Picton. Cocktail first?'

Damn it. I like the way he says that. It's such a formal name, but when he says it I sound like a courtesan or something.

'First?' I can't help teasing.

He drops the towel, hooking it around his body once more, and I'm glad even though it means I can't perve at him so easily. It stops my blood from simmering itself into a fever state.

'First. As in first, before I fuck you senseless.' He grins, pulling me to him.

Something about this feels so right, and it should feel wrong. And awkward. I shake my head, my eyes dropping to the floor before I remember that I've known Jack for two years and that whatever happens we work together and I won't be cowered by him and what we are.

'Cocktails sound perfect.'

His smile is a flicker and then, his eyes holding mine, his smile just a smudge across his handsome face, he lifts my dress with the same reverence a groom might lift his bride's veil and finds my nakedness.

He groans approvingly. 'You've been waiting for me all day?' His hands curve around my butt, pulling me tight to him.

'Well, you did tear my underpants,' I point out.

'Sorry about that.' His voice shows that he is anything but.

He releases me and I have to stifle a noise of impatience, watching as he saunters into the kitchen and pulls something from the freezer. It's a bottle, but I don't recognise it—nor the label. He shakes it, then opens the top. As he pours it into two glasses I realise that it has a thickened consistency, like a Frozen Coke.

I taste it tentatively, my eyes latched to his. 'Cherry?' I raise my brows, taking another sip.

'It's my new favourite flavour.'

My cheeks glow pink to rival the drink. 'Mine, too.'

'Good to see we're both re-evaluating our opinions,' he says with a wink. Then, almost as an afterthought, 'How was your day?'

'Busy.' I don't want to talk about work. We do enough of that. 'I spoke to my grandma and sat on the Heath, though.'

He laughs. 'Am I not giving you enough to do?'

I shoot him a look of dismissal. 'It was a short break.'

'I'm kidding.' His eyes are thoughtful. 'You never talk about your family.'

'Yes, I do,' I retort, perhaps too quickly. 'Just not with *you*.'

'I see. Why not?'

I'm pretty sure I'm scowling at him. 'Well, for starters, because up until recently our relationship has never remotely veered away from the professional...'

'That's not true. You've seen me naked. You wake me up most days.'

'Yes, I know.' Thoughts of his body sprawled over his bed make my blood simmer. 'You're my boss...'

'Then take it as a command.'

The thought of Jack commanding me is instantly memorable. My lungs are filled with thick, hot air.

'A *command*? You're my boss—not royalty.'

He shrugs. 'Is there a difference? Tell me about your grandmother.'

I laugh. A soft sound of disbelief. 'My grandmother? That's *really* what you want to talk about right now?'

'Why not?'

He sips his drink, his eyes locked to mine. It's a challenge! Just like always, he's finding my boundaries and pushing at them with a persistence I find hard to ignore. And I do like to rise to his challenges.

'Grandma is one of a kind,' I say after the smallest of pauses. 'Revolutionary. She worked until well into her seventies and has always been my biggest ally. She encourages me to push myself as hard as I can in everything I do.'

'What did she do?'

'For work? She was a nurse. Still is, actually.' My lips twitch. 'Just last month she saved a man in her nursing home after he had a heart attack. She threw off her cardigan and performed CPR until the staff got there.'

'Sounds like you're just as proud of her as she is of you.'

'Mmm...' I make a smooth noise of agreement, absent-mindedly running my fingers over the bones of my wrist.

His eyes catch the gesture and he steps around the bench towards me. Before I can guess what he's planning he dribbles some cherry daiquiri from his glass onto the skin I've just rubbed, then brings his lips to it, sucking it and kissing me gently.

'I'm sorry about this.'

Jack? Sorry? That's a novelty.

My heart squeezes at his gentle admission. My voice is soft when I speak. 'I told you, it doesn't hurt.'

'The bruising would say otherwise.'

I shrug, but the way his mouth is moving over me is making thought difficult. 'I'm fine. I would have told you if I didn't like it, believe me.'

'I do.'

He brings my thumb to his mouth and sucks on it. I shudder; the pleasure rips through me.

'So? What *do* you like? Usually?'

'With other men?' I clarify, and there is a strange darkening of his features before he wipes them clear and nods.

'Yes.'

I tilt my head to the side. 'Oh, you know—kinky shit.'

'Such as…?'

It's a calm, measured response beyond what I expect.

'I'll show you soon.'

He clears his throat. 'You bet your sweet arse, you will.' He grins and sips his drink once more.

'Anyway,' I ask throatily, 'what do *you* like? With other women? Or is the only prerequisite that they submit to your *wham-bam, thank you, ma'am* form of sex?'

He shakes his head. 'Not the *only* prerequisite, but it's an important one.'

'Why?' I push, taking another sip.

He presses his finger under my chin, tilting my face towards his. 'Because that's what I want.'

'One-night stands.'

'Two-night stands, in your case,' he says, pulling me forward.

At the same time I reach for his towel and push it down his body. He lifts me easily, settling me on a bar stool, his eyes holding mine as he slides on a condom, and then he takes me totally, driving deep inside me and winding my legs around his waist. Even as the bliss of his possession moves through me I feel a strange distaste for his statement.

A two-night stand on its second night means it's the end.

But don't I want that?

Aren't boundaries a *good* thing?

I bite down on my lip, unable to process it any more. He holds me tight, gripping me against him.

'I like being able to be inside you like this. Whenever I want.'

His fingers grab my dress and lift it up my body, over my head, so that I'm wearing only my heels and a lace bra. He disposes of the latter easily and then, true to his word, grabs his daiquiri glass and trickles ice-cold liquid across my breasts.

His mouth on my nipple is warm and I arch my back, giving him greater access. He chases it down my body as he thrusts into me again, his ownership of me both thrilling and frightening at the same time. His chin is stubbled and rough against my neck. He takes an earlobe into his mouth, wobbling it between his teeth, and I groan, desperate for him to move faster, deeper.

'What do you want?' he asks softly.

'More!' I call the word out loudly, an incantation or an invocation, scoring my nails across his back, marking him as mine even when I know he isn't.

'Like this?'

He moves a little deeper, so that I nod, but it's not enough.

'More...'

He laughs, pulling out of me and guiding me off the stool at the same time.

'Turn around.'

'Has anyone ever told you you're a bossy son of a bitch in bed?'

'We're not in bed,' he reminds me frankly, and there's a sexy, sardonic smile at the corner of his lips.

'You're a bossy son of a bitch to fuck,' I correct dutifully, and he laughs.

'You're complaining?'

I shoot him a look over my shoulder and do as he says, turning around.

'Those fucking heels...' he says, bending me at my waist and spreading my legs before taking me from behind, his fingers digging into my naked arse. 'You have no idea how hot this is.'

But I do, because he's driving me to the point of distraction with every single move. Fire spirals inside me, coiling, spinning, taking me and making me fall apart in his arms.

The kitchen bench is marble and cold beneath my fevered palms. And then he brings the palm of his hand down on my arse and I jerk, crying out as both pleasure and pain radiate through me.

'Did you know you have a mark here from me?' He

presses into what I presume must be a hickey from the last time we were together.

I shake my head and he catches my ponytail in his hand, pulling it with just enough pressure to hold me still as he thrusts inside me. His other hand trails down my spine, chasing each knot, each groove, until he reaches my arse. Once again he presses a single finger against me, and there is something so illicit and forbidden about it that I come—out of nowhere.

The orgasm is intense. He's only touching my skin, there is nothing invasive about his finger, but just the idea of what I'd let him do to me makes me fall apart.

'Shit…' I swear under my breath, sweat across my brow.

His finger pushes in a little way and I buck hard. His dick thrusts into me and his hand around my hair pulls. It's too much. The pleasure is making me weak.

'I can't…' I say, my breath coming in pants, my eyes fevered, my body wet.

'You can do whatever you want,' he contradicts, and brings his mouth to my back.

But he moves his hand away, bringing it to cup my breasts and torment my nipples. I have never known sex like this. I have never been an instrument of pleasure. I always call the shots and yet now I am his to control, to command, and there is something so hedonistic about that I know I will never be the same again.

'You are so much more perfect than I imagined,' he groans, and now he thrusts deeper and harder and faster, and I rock my hips with him until we fall apart together, him exploding inside me while I tremble and squeeze him tight.

I bring my weight forward, pressing my head onto the marble kitchen bench, not wanting to lose him.

He belongs inside me.

It's an erroneous thought. No one person can belong to another—inside or out.

'I needed that.'

He steps away from me as though he's sated, when I'm satisfied and still needy all at once.

'You and me both.'

I walk around the kitchen bench on legs that are wobbly as all hell. I sip some of my drink, my eyes linked to his. But he's staring at my breasts. Bemused, I look down and see that they're red from his stubble.

His jaw is clenched and he looks away.

Something jars in my mind. A memory I can't quite grab, like finding soap in the bath.

'What is it?'

His smile is tight. 'I ordered Japanese.'

'Great. No karaoke, though,' I tease, referring to my last drunken night with Jack.

He nods. But something is wrong.

'What is it?' I insist.

'I've marked your entire body,' he says after a beat has passed. 'You're literally covered in marks from me.'

I frown, running my hands over my breasts, and then I shrug. 'So?'

His eyes, when they meet mine, are haunted. 'It doesn't bother you that I *like* fucking marking you? That I'm turned on by seeing proof of me on you?'

I tilt my head to one side, pretending bemusement, but my heart is accelerating and again I wonder at the risk of broken ribs in the face of a particularly aggressive heartbeat.

I shake my head slowly.

'Jesus…' He drags a hand through his hair unsteadily. 'All this time I thought you were Miss Moneypenny and you're actually Air Force Amy.'

'Who?'

He doesn't answer, just reaches down and picks up his towel, wrapping it around his waist, then walks into the kitchen to stand behind me. He runs his finger down my spine.

'There is a line here.' He drops his finger lower and presses it against my butt. 'And here, where I sucked you until you bruised.' Then he cups my arse. 'And here, where I slapped you hard enough to redden your skin.'

I swallow. This description of his touch is erotic and dangerous.

I suck my lip between my teeth. 'Don't you get it?' I don't look at him as I speak. 'When I'm here, I'm yours. I trust you. And I want this. This—what you do to me—is what turns me on. More than anything I've ever known.'

He drops his forehead to my shoulder, and then he grabs me and turns me around to face him. 'It doesn't bother you that I'm just using you?'

It's not what I expect him to say. I look at him with an obvious expression of confusion because he shakes his head.

'Not *you*, per se. Sex with you.'

I try to play the lighter side. 'Do I seem like I mind?'

He exhales, frustration and anger communicating themselves in the weighted breath. 'I don't want you to be another one of *them*.'

His eyes are hollow. No matter how I stare at him, I can't intuit his meaning.

'Another one of whom?'

'Them. The women I fuck to forget about her.'

I know instantly that he's referring to Lucy. Sadness wells inside me. Sadness for Jack, for Lucy and the whole sordid mess.

'But that's all this can be.'

There's a determination in his statement that fills me with ice.

I nod, but his words are exploding in my mind like tiny little bombs.

'I know,' I say. Because I do.

That's the worst thing. I have known this about him for a long time and yet here I am, fucking him and letting him drive me crazy when I should be running a mile in the opposite direction.

'So what are you doing here? How can you be okay with that?'

A great fucking question! One I wish I'd asked myself sooner.

'Hasn't that horse already bolted? We've had sex together. Does it really matter why?'

'I don't know.' His laugh is uncertain, his eyes cagey. 'I'm not usually this...*barbaric*.'

He drops his mouth to my shoulder and bites me gently.

'But with you...I don't know...it's like some animal instinct kicks in. I feel like I want to carry you over my shoulder and tie you to my bed.'

'You've already done that. Check and check.'

A flicker of his lips acknowledges the truth of my reply. 'I mean for days. I mean I want to feed you when it suits me. Let you drink the champagne that I tip into your mouth. But otherwise you'd exist for my pleasure alone.'

'Maybe you just want that because you know I'd never go for it,' I say hoarsely, hiding the fact that his words have evoked a powerful emotional need in me.

'Maybe.'

Suddenly, his need gives me an idea. No, it gives me a bartering chip. 'What if I let you go all Neanderthal?'

'You think I haven't already?' he asks, the words full of hoarse self-condemnation.

I shake my head. 'I think you've just scratched the surface.' I cup his face, rubbing my thumb over his stubble. 'So give me what I want and I'll give you what you want.'

'And what *is* it you want, Gemma Picton?'

I swallow my anxiety. What's the worst that can happen? He'll say no?

'I want you to answer my questions. I want to understand you better.'

The shower is warm against my skin. I rub my body all over, letting the soap bubble and froth before turning the heat off and stepping out into an enormous soft towel. I dry myself and then reach for one of the luxurious robes hanging behind the door.

I'm nervous, as though I'm on a first date. But that's stupid.

Because Jack doesn't date. Come to think of it, I don't really date either.

What we're doing is fucking—sure, the best sex of my life. But still just sex. Two nights? Maybe more? But definitely not any form of happily-ever-after.

It's sex. And it's discovery.

I'm getting my curiosity answered—and I have been curious about Jack for as long as I've worked with him. I've wondered about the demons that drive him. The ghosts, real and imagined, that play on the edges of his mind.

Besides, it's kind of win-win for me. I love the animal passion in him. So much so I'm terrified of myself. This way I get to find out more about the beautiful darkness of Jack Grant, and I get the beast in bed.

Perfect.

When I step out of the bathroom he's arranging containers on an enormous dining table. It could easily seat twelve people, but he's placed us at one end and, in a gesture that makes my heart thump, he's even lit a candle.

'Expecting company?' I murmur with forced sarcasm, desperate to cover the trembling emotion in my chest.

'That's not what I'd call you,' he responds in kind, but he winks at me and my heart pounds harder.

'We've covered that already with—who was it? Amy someone?'

He grins. 'I called you Miss Moneypenny first.'

'Yes, and that's equally wrong. I'm not some wall-flower assistant.'

'You assist me,' he says with a shrug, but he comes to a chair and pulls it out, his eyes meeting mine, silently inviting me to sit.

Electricity sparks between us like a current neither of us can control.

I'm nervous, and that makes me angry! I don't want to be nervous around Jack, like this is a date or something. I've agreed to let him ravage me so that he'll tell me stuff. It's not a date. If it were he'd tell me all that stuff without the promise of animalistic sex.

It's only when I sit that I pay attention to the kind of food he's ordered. There's sushi, sashimi, a Katsu curry, edamame and a couple of miso soups. I try not to think he's remembered that Katsu curry is my favourite thing in the world.

He takes the seat opposite mine and lifts a glass. I tilt mine towards his and then rest it back on the table.

'It's bad luck not to drink after clinking glasses.'

'I haven't heard that.'

I lift the drink to my lips and taste it. Of course it's delicious.

He rests back in the chair, his hands linked beneath his chin. 'Well, Miss Picton. We have a deal. What is it you'd like to know?'

'You'll tell me anything?'

'And you'll let me *do* anything.'

I nod, my throat dry as I wonder just what his idea of 'anything' encompasses.

'How do you know I won't chicken out, out of interest?'

His laugh makes my gut vibrate. 'Because you're you. I can't imagine you backing away from anything in your life. You're fearless.'

'Not entirely,' I say under my breath.

'No? What are you afraid of?'

I sip my wine again, and then snap my chopsticks in half reaching for a piece of salmon *nigiri*. 'I'm afraid of lightning,' I say softly. 'Terrified of it.'

'As in thunder and lightning?'

I nod. 'Yep. That one.'

'But why? It's just atmospheric discharge.'

'Yeah. It's just a weather phenomenon. But I will still hide under my covers during a storm, waiting for it to pass, without fail.'

'Why? Since when?'

My smile is lopsided. 'Since I was a girl.'

'What happened?'

'How do you know *anything* happened?'

'I just do,' he says with a shrug of his broad shoulders, lifting his own chopsticks and taking a piece of chicken *karaage*.

He's right, of course.

'I was seven years old and locked out of our home. I'd gone to pick apples and my parents presumed I was in bed. They were out to dinner with friends and Nanny Winters thought I'd gone with them. The house was locked up and I couldn't get in.'

I shiver. It was one of the most horrifying nights I can recall.

'I climbed into my tree house and waited it out there. But a flash of lightning came down so close and so loud it smoked on the ground at my feet.'

He nods thoughtfully, but I can tell he's unravelling the story.

'When did you get back into your home?'

'Not until morning. I fell asleep eventually, and it wasn't until Nanny discovered me missing and the alarm was raised that I heard the staff looking for me. I woke up and all was well. Except that I can't stand storms now. Even the smell of rain in the air makes me afraid.'

He strokes his chin thoughtfully.

'So I'm not entirely fearless,' I finish lamely.

'Lots of people are afraid of thunderstorms.'

'Are *you*?'

'No.' His smile is perfunctory. 'There isn't much I'm afraid of.'

'But...?' I ask, sipping my wine, curious to the point of distraction.

'Yes, I have fears,' he admits grudgingly.

'Like...?'

He makes a deep, guttural noise. 'This was a crappy idea.'

I laugh softly. 'Ghosts? Spiders?'

'No.' He's quiet for so long I wonder if he's not going to answer, and then he continues, his voice hoarse. 'I'm afraid of powerlessness. Of watching someone I love die.'

His grief hits me like a web and I am caught in it.

'You've watched someone you love die and you've survived.'

'Barely.' He shakes his head. 'Try the chicken. It's great.'

I don't move. The ghosts of his admission linger between us, haunting our table.

'Were you with her when she died?'

He recoils as though he's been slapped and I briefly regret the agreement we've made. But I want to *know* this stuff. It's so important to me to understand. I feel like I've got only half of the picture and bit by bit I want to piece him together.

'Yes.'

'I'm sorry.'

'I wanted to be with her.'

'Of course.' I nod. 'How long were you married?'

'A year.' He clears his throat. 'Can we talk about something else?'

Sympathy is thick inside of me but instinctively I

know talking about this will help him so I don't back down. 'You told me I could ask what I want.'

'And this is what you want to know?'

'You told me you're fucking me because of her—so, yes, I want to know.'

His face pales. 'Fine.' His teeth are gritted. 'What else?'

I drink some wine and eat another piece of sushi, chewing on it thoughtfully. 'She died of cancer?'

He nods.

'And...?' I prompt.

'And *what*, Gemma?'

'Well, what kind?'

He expels an angry breath. 'Chronic Lymphocytic Leukaemia. Stage Four. It was a terminal diagnosis.'

I wince. 'I'm so sorry.'

'Why? It's not your fault.'

I understand his anger and aggression.

'Nothing could be done?'

His eyes meet mine and he shakes his head. I feel like he's holding something back, but I don't want to push him anymore. Not about this.

Sympathy trumps curiosity. So I let it go.

'This is delicious,' I say instead, reaching for another piece.

And he visibly relaxes, as though he's been in hell and I'm unlocking the gate.

'Yeah.'

'Do you spend much time here?' I look around the palatial apartment, seeing it almost as if for the first time.

'I used to.' His smile is tight. 'So...Nanny Winters, huh?'

'No, no—*you* don't get to change the subject.'

He laughs. 'I can do what I want.'

'That's not our deal.'

'Your parents worked full-time?'

It's so like Jack to push on with his line of questioning just because it suits him.

I stare at him. 'Not really.'

'Yet you were raised by a nanny?'

'I had three nannies,' I say, grabbing a piece of avocado sushi and eating it, then sipping my wine. 'Nanny Winters oversaw the other two.'

'*Three* nannies?' His voice is bordering on a scoff. 'So you were a handful even as a child?'

I roll my eyes. 'Did you not hear my thunderstorm story?'

'A runaway and a handful?' He nods with mock seriousness.

'Yep.'

'Your parents were rich?'

'*Are* rich,' I agree.

'Funny… I didn't have you picked as the daughter of some loaded guy.'

I arch a brow teasingly. 'Technically I'm the daughter of a loaded guy *and* a loaded lady. Duchess Arabella Picton, in fact.'

'No shit? *That* I did not see coming.'

He laughs then—a sound that relaxes me because it's so like us to laugh together that I am reminded of the years we've spent working together, getting to know one another. Not like this, admittedly, but in a different way.

'Why not?' I ask.

He laughs again and my gut clenches.

'So you slaving away for me is like a vanity job?'

I frown. 'No!'

'But you're going to inherit a fortune?'

I shrug, deciding it's better not to talk about my trust fund with Jack. I figure he won't really appreciate the amount that's sitting in my name in a Swiss bank account.

'One day.'

'Fascinating.'

'Not really.'

He nods, but I can see the wheels of his brain turning. 'You studied law, right?'

I roll my eyes. 'I'm your in-house counsel, what do you think?'

He grins and my tummy tilts off-balance. 'I don't pay too much attention to what my assistants do at university.'

I shoot him a look of disapproval but bite my tongue. He's goading me, and I won't give him the satisfaction of knowing he's been successful. 'I studied law and economics at Oxford, thank you very much.'

'Let me guess...you did well?'

My gaze doesn't falter. 'Double first.'

He tilts his head back, his laugh a soft caress. 'Not at all surprising.'

'How do you not know this about me? You hired me to work for you.'

'Yeah... Expecting you to last about three seconds.'

'Really? Why?'

'Because that's how long all my other assistants lasted.'

I grit my teeth. 'Counsels.'

'Your job is pretty much unfillable.'

'Because you're such a charm to work with,' I point out.

'Whatever the reason, no one stays around. So why have you?'

'Because I like a challenge,' I say honestly, my chin jutting out, my eyes holding to his. And he is still. Watchful. The air between us thickens.

'I'm a challenge?'

I laugh. 'You're kidding, right?'

He reaches for a piece of sushi. I watch him eat it and my stomach squeezes. How can I want him again already? I am fire and flame, bursting with need.

'Were you always like this? Or is it just since… Lucy?'

He frowns and doesn't answer right away. I can practically see the cogs turning in his brain. 'I don't know.'

'Well, before she…she died, did you have a con-stantly changing stream of staff?'

He shrugs. 'No.'

I nod, slowly. So this *is* a hangover of Lucy's death. My job, my being here, it all comes back to her. To Lucy.

The emotional strangulation of that is not something I think I'll easily comprehend, and so I stand up slowly.

'I've had enough for now.' My eyes meet his and now I am the one issuing a challenge. 'So show me.'

'Show you what?' he asks with a purposeful glint in his eye.

'Show me what *you* want.'

CHAPTER SEVEN

I'M IN LIMBO.

Not asleep…not awake. I lie in his bed, my body throbbing with pleasures untold, my mind exhausted.

It is late. Somewhere between midnight and dawn. And I am his.

I lift up on one elbow, my eyes hazy as I look down at him. He is beautiful and he is sexy. He is groggy. Almost asleep. But his eyes flick to mine and I see blank speculation in them.

Confusion.

Wariness.

'How are you?'

I smile—I hope it's as reassuring as I intend and not maniacal as I suspect. 'Good.'

He nods tersely, pushing up out of bed, dragging a hand through his hair as he stalks across to his wardrobe. He emerges after a moment, boxer shorts on. At least he's not showering me away immediately.

But he will soon enough. I know Jack too well to misunderstand his mood now, and it pisses me off as much as it worries me. I don't want a relationship, but I don't know how we can go from white-hot sex to awkward silence in the space of minutes.

'Do you need anything?' His voice is husky. 'Drink? Coffee? Shower?'

A flicker of annoyance draws my lips into a frown. 'No, thanks.'

I stand up, feeling as though I've run ten marathons. My body is sore and stiff, but still throbbing with pleasures previously unknown. My dress is—where? Out in the living area?

I walk towards him slowly, and pause just in front of him. What *he* wants is crystal-clear; my own needs are far more difficult to interpret but I *do* want to interpret them.

Self-preservation draws me inwards, away from Jack before he can push me away. 'I'm going to go.'

I see the emotions that flicker on his face and I recognise only one—relief.

'Are you sure?'

I laugh—a soft sound that covers whatever that heavy pain is in my chest. 'Come on, Jack. We both know how this works.'

I press a kiss against his cheek and move into the lounge. Our sushi feast is still on the table—a relic of our attempt at a date. Like normal people date. But we're *not* normal. Not on our own and definitely not together. We're misfits, both of us, operating outside the normal realms of this kind of relationship thing.

I scoop up my dress and bra and pull the dress on over my naked body, stuffing the bra into my handbag as I step into my shoes.

My hair I pull over one shoulder, brushing my fingers through its tangled length to neaten it somewhat.

'Martins will be on roster now,' he says, looking at the clock over the oven and referring to one of the junior staff drivers.

I shake my head. The last thing I want is for a company driver to see me like this, post-Jack-Grant-ravaging. 'I'll get a cab.' I walk towards him again and press a single kiss to his cheek.

'I'll see you Monday.'

'Monday…' He nods and there are more emotions in his face, these harder to comprehend. 'Right. It's the weekend.'

I swallow past a lump in my throat. 'And then Australia,' I remind him—probably unnecessarily.

'Yeah.'

His eyes probe mine. I feel like I'm escaping prison and one of those enormous floodlights has landed on me, full beam.

'You're okay?'

'I'm fine,' I reassure him.

We've just had pretty much the best sex in the world—I doubt it has ever been better for anyone than it is for us. But I know I need to go. It's important. My self-preservation instincts are blaring loudly, demanding I put some space between us.

He nods, and it's only then that I realise he's got a glass of Scotch in his hand.

It hurts. There's something about seeing him with a drink that reminds me of what he does—how often he does it and how he reacts afterwards. And I don't want that to be the case with us.

Those self-preservation instincts join forces with my brain and they pull the strings to make me smile brightly.

'Thanks for tonight. I had fun. See you soon.'

And I turn and walk slowly towards the door, my heart thudding, my mind foggy.

* * *

I watch her leave with a certainty that I'm messing up my life in a monumental way. What the *hell* am I doing? Sleeping with Gemma *once* was a disastrous cock-up. But again and again? Showing her all my dark spaces and hauntings?

No one needs to know the demons that lash me.

I am in control. That's me. It's the persona I've built and I don't like the idea of someone knowing that it's not completely true. Lucy knew, of course. And I guess Amber does; she's seen me in a pretty fucked-up state, right after Lucy died. But Gemma? Now?

Her eyes, big and intelligent, are assessing, always understanding. And the way her face scrunches when she's about to come... The way her body trembles beneath mine... Jesus. I want her now—again—more.

I turn to the door. If I chased her what would she say? God, would she think it means I want more than sex? Ironic, given that I *just* want sex. With Gemma.

An obsession is building inside me. Bit by bit it is closing me in. But Gemma Picton is hardly going to let me turn her into my own personal sex slave. Although I think she's about as caught up in all of this as I am...

All the more reason for me to fight harder, to control it.

I grip the crystal tumbler in my hands, feeling my anger and determination surge, and I pitch the glass hard against the wall. It breaks with satisfying immediacy, shattering into thousands of tiny pieces that mix with the slosh of amber liquid running fast down the wall before landing with a thud against the tiles. I drag my hand through my hair and stare at the destruction with a sense of satisfaction.

I'm good at ruining things. At breaking them.

That's what I need to stick to.

I don't think I'll ever eat again. Grandma has no such qualms. She reaches for another oyster—it must be her tenth—and swirls it inside lips she's painted bright red for the occasion.

'What's in Australia?'

I stare out at the little street, watching a small black car reverse—badly—into a narrow parking space. 'Work.'

'Always work…' She sighs.

I nod absently.

Jack will be there, too. After not going to Tokyo, I don't suppose there's the smallest hope I can get out of it.

'I promise I'll do something fun. Just for you.'

My insides quiver as I imagine what that could be. *Jack*. Doing Jack would be fun.

But even as my pulse is stirring and my heart is beginning to race my brain is demonstratively reminding me of Jack's particular brand of cold fishery. His ability to walk away from me right after we've shared mind-blowing, simultaneous orgasms is as offensive as it is unique.

Am I crazy to be letting this happen?

Yes, hisses my brain. *He's told you he's using you. He still loves his dead wife. Jesus. You're a fool.*

'Grandma…' I pause, my lips tight as I dismiss whatever the heck I'd been about to say.

She swallows the oyster—Grandma is the only person I know who actually chews the slimy little devils first...*shudder*...like phlegmatic explosions...*ugh*. Her gaze is cool and direct.

At eighty, Grandma is every bit as beautiful as she was in her youth. Lined, ephemeral and pale now, but with a glimmer in her eyes, a wave to her silver shoulder-length hair and a smile that is punctuated by straight white teeth—all her own. Her nose is straight, her eyes wide-set, her figure as svelte as ever. And she dresses in a fashion which somehow straddles the latest in trends without coming across as an attempt to be youthful.

'Something's on your mind.'

I shake my head and reach for my bread roll. Only I've already fingered it anxiously, reducing it to a pile of wheaten crumbs and ash.

'When Grandpa died, did you think about finding someone else?'

She snorts. 'There is no one else.'

The words make me smile, yet they are also sounding the death knell for the hope I hadn't realised I've been carrying.

'No one?' I tease.

'No one.' She expels a sigh. 'Your grandfather was... What we shared is impossible to explain.' She sips her champagne, her eyes growing even more intensely watchful, if that's possible. 'Have I ever told you about how we met?'

I shake my head, even though I know the story backwards.

'Liar!' She chuckles.

We're interrupted by a waiter, but Grandma dispenses with him quickly, placing an order for another bottle of champagne and then fixing me with that steady grey gaze of hers.

'He was sitting on the lawns at Huntington, his knees bent, his chin resting on them. His face was resolutely turned away from me, but as I approached his eyes shifted, locking to my face. It was as if he was telling me all his secrets and begging me to help him in that one single second. He looked at me as if he knew that I was the only person on earth who would be able to dig through his shit and find the kernel of the boy he'd once been.'

Grandma is looking over my shoulder now. The story is one she's told so many times that it comes out word for word as I remember it. Still, I lean forward, the invisible threads of magic and history curling around me.

'That enormous oak tree was just to his side—far enough away to prevent shade from darkening him, but close enough to dwarf him. He was a big man, your grandfather. Tall and strong—built for battle.' Her lips twist with undisguised disgust. 'But not strong in spirit. His spirit had been broken and the tree made that obvious to me.'

Her eyes flick back to mine and I feel it, too. Just like she did. The weight of silent communication and understanding.

'I loved him instantly.'

My heart does a weird little palpitation in my chest. 'I can't imagine that.'

'Why?'

'It's just unfathomable to me.'

'That's because you haven't met someone worth loving yet,' she says with a shrug of her elegant shoulders. 'One day you'll know just what I mean.'

I quirk my lips, hoping my smile seems dismissive. My pulse has speeded up. I try to quell it.

'I don't think it always works like that.'

'Perhaps not. Your grandfather *was* special.'

'What you shared was special,' I murmur, reaching across and squeezing her hand.

Grandma's eyes flicker, her lips tighten and she nods, as if to dismiss the conversation. The waiter appears, brandishing a bottle of champagne, and begins to unfurl the foil top. Grandma stares resolutely at the view as the waiter performs his ministrations, and doesn't smile when he pours two fresh glasses.

She is very much the Duchess in instances like this: a woman who has become so used to service and being served that it isn't even an act she needs to be grateful for.

I smile my thanks as he leaves.

Grandma waits until we are alone again. 'You will never meet anyone—no lover, no special friend, no one—if you are behind your desk all day.'

Out of nowhere I picture Jack. I picture the way he drapes himself against the doorframe, the way his body is so languid and sensual, and my stomach flops.

'Have I told you the foundation is almost ready to launch?'

Grandma tilts her head to one side. 'I admire your commitment to that...' she says, clearly trying to frame whatever she's thinking carefully. 'But you have money. If philanthropy is your aim, why not set up your own charity?'

'Perhaps I will—one day. But my job is more than

just one thing… You know that.' I expel a sigh, frustration gnawing at me. 'You've always championed my work.'

'You're very clever. And I know you're brilliant at what you do. But you're sacrificing too much now. I championed your work because I hoped you would find a way to pursue your career and still live your life. You, more than anyone I've ever known, have the ability to keep multiple balls in the air at once. So why aren't you doing it?'

I drop my head, my eyes not meeting hers. There is so much truth in what she's saying, but the criticism hurts.

'I…I am.' It's a lie. We both know that. But reality is not something I want to face.

'*All* of you is focussed on that job. On that man. I'm worried you're going to wake up one day and realise what you've sacrificed. And all for *him*.'

My heart bumps against my ribs, banging them with its frantic racing. 'He's brilliant.'

'And a bastard, by all reports.'

Yes. A beautiful, arrogant, brilliant, sex-obsessed bastard.

Was it only yesterday he was inside me? It feels like forever ago. I am at a fever pitch of want—want only he can answer. My insides clench instantly, remembering him, needing him, craving his touch, smell and taste…

'He's not that bad.' The words are hoarse, punctured by breath and memory.

'With him and that job in your life you're never going to be truly happy.'

Her pronouncement is spoken in a way that is almost prophetic. A shiver dances down my spine, spiralling coldness across my flesh like a breath from the North Pole.

'Travelling and living off the family trust would be better?' I arch a brow. 'You know me better than that. I *live* for what I do. I *love* it. Maybe *that's* the love of my life.'

Silence prickles between us. Silence that is suffocating and unwelcome.

'Very well,' she clips, dismissing this conversation, as well. 'I don't like the way they've trimmed those hedges. It's so severe.'

I breathe again, but my heart is still twisting and thumping. The truth sits heavily in my mind but I step away from it.

There is no ulterior motive to my working so hard for Jack. There's no mystery as to why I don't feel like I've sacrificed a damn thing for him. It doesn't mean anything that I am fulfilled and alive, energised every time I speak to him, see him, do his bidding. But my stomach drops. Because actually I think there probably *is* a meaning—just one I don't want to appreciate. *Fuck.*

His jet is the last word in space-age luxury. Cream leather armchairs on either side of the aisle, thick carpet a pale beige and lamps that would look at home in a five-star hotel make the perfect night-flight reading environment. USB docks are in every armrest to charge phones and iPads, and there are several bedrooms, a boardroom and a small cinema.

There is also a brooding billionaire sitting at the back of the plane, his head bent over a stack of files, apparently engrossed.

I ignore him. Or pretend to.

We've hardly spoken since I left his apartment on Friday night.

That was easy enough over the weekend. After sharing two bottles of champagne and being drilled in life's lessons, Grandma and I shopped in the high street, selecting a new clutch purse for Grandma to take to the anniversary dinner and pretending we weren't both dreading the damned thing.

I didn't hear from Jack, and it wasn't until I got back to my own place on Sunday evening that I realised I'd been expecting to. That I'd thought he'd text or call or email or something.

Those two days away from him, without seeing him, stretched interminably.

The knowledge prickled down my spine so that on Monday morning I steeled myself to be as standoffish and unaffected as possible. To fight coldness with cool unconcern, with no care.

But I didn't see him then either. He arrived late, left early and didn't speak to me.

And I didn't speak to him, despite the fact I needed his signature on some papers.

I chickened out and actually hid from him when he walked past my office, ducking beneath my desk.

Crazy, right?

Not so much.

We've moved into dangerous territory. I don't know if he realises it, but there are warnings blaring in my head. I don't want to need Jack Grant like I do. I don't mean sexually. I mean in every way.

Only I can't imagine my life without him.

We've been flying for the better part of a day now,

and hardly spoken beyond a perfunctory, polite 'Hiya' as he boarded the flight, ten minutes late and looking like sex and seduction in a ten-thousand-pound suit.

I have been telling myself I don't care with varying measures of success. Did I expect he'd storm up to me and kiss me? Take me passionately in his arms and hold me close? Tell me he never wants to go three days without seeing me again?

He's made it abundantly clear what he wants.

It should be what I want, too.

I shut my eyes for a moment, crossing my legs in the armchair, and am surprised when I'm woken a moment later.

'We're landing.' Jack's hands are at my hips and I bat them away instinctively.

He grabs the seatbelt and clips it across me—tight—his eyes flicking to mine. The hint of a smile on his face makes my heart flip-flop.

'Have I ever told you that you snore?'

Warmth invades my face. 'I know. I have mild asthma.'

He grins and takes the seat beside mine. My body is instantly aware of him and my brain is pretty pissed off at the rapid response.

I shift a little, looking down at my watch. I must have slept for over an hour. I blink, opening the world clock function on my phone. It's six o'clock in Sydney, which means I want to be tired—not refreshed after a quick nap on the flight.

Silence stretches between us. Debbie, one of his flight attendants, clips out efficiently, 'We'll be touching down on schedule. Can I get you anything before we land?'

'Water, thanks.' I smile at her, turning my attention back to the papers I'd been reading.

Well, half my attention. A quarter of it. A sliver. The tiny part that's not completely drawn to Jack and his nearness and his hypermasculine fragrance. The part of me that isn't all wrapped up in the way he's sitting, legs spread, arms relaxed, body warm and large and so close I could push out of my seat and sit on his lap. Unzip his pants and take him.

God. I want that.

'Dr Pepper.'

His response to Debbie's question shakes the desire from my mind, but he looks at me and my toes curl. Does he guess what I'm thinking?

I tap my pen against the side of the page I'm reading in an attempt to focus my thoughts in a more appropriate direction.

But Jack reaches across, his hand curling over mine. My pulse goes into overdrive.

'Did you have a good weekend?' he asks.

I laugh. I can't help it. A short, sharp sound of weary frustration. 'Yeah.'

He nods, and a frown pulls at his lips. 'I don't know how to speak to you now.'

And I feel sorry for him. Sorry for me. Because we're both in the middle of a patch of uncertainty too wide to navigate.

'I'm still me.'

'But it's different.'

'Yeah… I don't know if you ever asked me about my weekend before we had sex together.'

I lower my voice as Debbie walks back into the

cabin. She places a glass of water on my side table and a can of soda on Jack's.

As Debbie disappears once more he winks at me. 'It's cherry flavour.'

Damn him. He knows what he's doing to me.

My pulse fires and I give him a tight half-smile before returning my attention to the document I'm partway through reading.

'You've got a breakfast meeting at seven o'clock with the mayor. While you're with him I'm going to be going over the premises. Then I'll meet with your Australian CEO, Clint Sheridan, to touch base on recruitment matters. The broker for the New Zealand deal is meeting us for lunch at Aria, and Clint's asked you to his place for dinner, with a few of the other executives.'

'Asked *us*, you mean,' he corrects, his eyes hooked to mine.

I frown. 'It's just social. You don't need me—'

'I want you there,' he says firmly, and I remember that he *is* actually my boss.

Plus, if it weren't for the fact that we've had sex I wouldn't have ever thought of *not* going. It's my own way of not blurring the lines, but he sees right through it.

'You've done most of this deal. You *should* be there.'

I pull my lips to the side thoughtfully. 'Sure.'

It's not worth arguing about. We've gone to hundreds of this kind of thing in our time. I'm sure this won't be any different.

He nods, but he's distracted. 'Do we need to talk?'

His suggestion sets off a kaleidoscope of possibilities. Talk? About what? About us? What would I say? And him?

I swallow to hide my confusion and return his question with one of my own. 'Do we?'

He reaches across and wipes his thumb over my lip. Butterflies bounce around my gut.

'I guess not. It doesn't matter.'

I stare straight ahead, moving out of his reach. Because maybe this *doesn't* matter. Maybe this is just one of those things and in a few weeks I'll wonder what the heck I got so worked up about. Why I let him get under my skin like this.

I hope it's true even as I know how unlikely that is.

CHAPTER EIGHT

I LOVE AUSTRALIA. We don't get here often—though with Jack opening this office that will probably change.

The heat and humidity hit me as soon as the doors open. Even in the air-conditioned airport there's a sultry oppressiveness that makes me ache to find the nearest swimming pool and dive straight in.

A limo is waiting for us, and a couple of reporters from the broadsheet newspapers. I forget sometimes that Jack is a 'Person of Interest', especially in the business world. Working with him for over two years has made him just 'Jack' to me, but to the world he's an enigmatic tycoon and philanthropist.

I remember feeling awestruck before I knew him. The prospect of working for him was one I pinned all my hopes to.

Now it's just my life.

Jack and I have been pretty much inseparable this whole time. I'm his right hand. Despite having been hired as his in-house counsel, my job has morphed and varied and now incorporates a wide variety of duties. I'm across his workload and can step in at any point, finishing negotiations, speaking on his behalf. When we travel together we either stay in adjoining rooms or in one of his apartments. It depends on how long we're in town and what's required of us.

This unfettered access has been helpful when we needed to proof things late at night or discuss early morning meetings. It's never been an issue. But the thought of sharing his penthouse at Woolloomooloo is filling me with a sense of apprehension. Not because I'm afraid of him. I'm afraid of what I want from him—what I need. Of what living in close confines, even temporarily, will force us to confront.

My sense of foreboding doesn't improve once we arrive and I remember how stunning the place is. How glamorous and romantic.

The thought is errant and I quash it immediately. Romance be damned. We're colleagues who happen to be sleeping together. That's all.

The penthouse is in a big converted wharf building. He bought the whole top floor from some Hollywood celebrity about five years ago, converting several luxurious flats into one enormous sky home. It has panoramic views of Sydney Harbour. From where I'm standing I can see the bridge and a beautiful little island. There's a balcony that wraps all the way around and a lap pool in a glass room to one side.

I look at the water, my temptation obvious.

'Plans for tonight?'

Jack's right behind me. I don't turn around but I can feel his nearness. My body quivers; I want to jump him.

'None. Getting into the time zone.'

'I'm *in* the time zone, baby.' He grins, and strolls towards the enormous glass windows that overlook the harbour. 'I'm also hungry enough to eat a horse.' He turns to face me, his eyes dragging from my head to my toes and then back up, slowing down over my cleavage. 'Shall we go out?'

My body is sticky from the humidity and I am weary. Wary, too. Instinctively I understand that we need to keep some boundaries in place. Going out, just the two of us, is an unacceptable boundary erosion.

I smile—hopefully politely. 'I'm going to have a swim before I do another thing. Don't feel you have to wait for me to eat.'

I walk back towards the door, to where our suitcases are, and wheel mine along beside me down the corridor.

I find the room I used last time I was here and step into it, shutting the door behind me with an emphatic click. I lean against it and suck in a deep breath, then open the case and pull out my swimsuit. A simple black one-piece. I slip it on, pausing to check my reflection before wrapping a towel around my middle and walking back into the apartment.

I hear him before I see him and my stomach twists. His powerful arms are pulling him through the water, and if you told me he had trained as an Olympic swimmer I would believe you. His tan glistens like gold beneath the Australian sun.

Trying valiantly to ignore the heat between my legs, I drop my towel onto a lounger and dive in, long and low, holding my breath for as long as I can before kicking to the surface and swimming all the way to the end. I rest my arms on the sun-warmed coping and stare out at the harbour beneath us.

It looks like someone has shattered a thousand diamonds and thrown them over the water's top. The way it glistens is almost impossible to believe.

He swims up beside me. 'You're angry at me.'

He doesn't touch me, but the words feel like finger-prints on my chest.

I turn to him slowly, my hair wet, my eyes sur-rounded by clumps of black lashes. 'No.'

His expression is one of impatience. 'I'm no good at this. Tell me what I've done so I know.'

'What you've *done*?' It's so ludicrous that I almost laugh, but an equal urge to cry rises in my chest. 'You haven't "done" anything, Jack. I thought we'd agreed that this is our deal? Sex—fine. Work—fine. Nothing in between.'

But out of nowhere I remember the way my grandma talks about meeting Grandpa. I look at Jack and my heart hammers. *Damn it.*

He stares back at me. I can practically see the cogs turning. 'You're in your late twenties?'

'Twenty-six,' I clarify, and the distinction is a small but important one, for some absurd reason I can't com-prehend. Am I vain about my age? *Really?*

'And you've never been in a relationship?'

'Why do you say that?' I ask, though he's right.

'I just don't see you as someone's girlfriend.'

'Gee, thanks,' I mutter, turning my attention back to the view.

His fingertip on my shoulder is so light that I al-most wonder if I've imagined his touch. But then he runs it down my wet arm, all the way to my elbow, and cups me there, squeezing gently. I turn towards him once more and he pushes out from the wall of the pool, bringing me with him, deeper into the water.

I'm a good swimmer, and I tread water without his help. But he stays close, his handsome face mesmeris-ing me with ocean-green eyes and darkly tanned skin.

'Am I wrong?'

I shake my head. 'Not necessarily.' A smile flicks across my lips without my permission. 'I've dated. And been with men when it's suited me. But I've always had demanding jobs, and not a lot of time to do the whole dinner-and-a-movie thing.'

He laughs. 'That sounds boring as shit.'

My thoughts exactly. 'How did you meet her?'

I don't need to say his wife's name. We both know who I mean. He expels a breath and looks away, his jaw clenched.

'It's fine if you don't want to talk about it,' I say, making to swim away, but he grabs my wrist and pulls me towards him. And I'm glad. I need him to need me, and it's a sign that he does. My heart smiles.

'You keep running away from me when you don't get your own way—did you know that?'

Do I? 'I'm not running away. I'm swimming away,' I say, in a very lame attempt at humour. 'And it's not because I don't get my own way—it's because talking to you is like talking to a brick wall. It's easy to…to run away when you're being pushed.'

His eyes widen in non-verbal acknowledgement of the point I've made. 'She was working at a restaurant in Edinburgh.' His eyes flash with remembered pain. 'I'd just wrapped up a meeting and was heading to the hotel. Thought I'd stop for a late dinner.' He clears his throat, but his voice is still gravelly. 'And I saw her.'

Jealousy fires inside me at the look of total wonderment that briefly crosses his eyes.

'She was finishing up and I made her nervous as hell.'

'Nervous? Why?'

Though, I remember belatedly my first meeting with Jack and the trepidation that lived in me. I hid it beneath a layer of finely honed bravado but, yes, I was nervous, too. He has a machismo and dynamism that is at once overpowering. I have truly never met anyone like him.

'She hadn't had a lot of good experience with men,' he says tightly, a muscle jerking in his square jaw.

'I'm sorry for that,' I say quietly.

'Yeah. I was, too.' His smile was haunted. 'The guy she'd left just before meeting me seemed to have thought of her as his own personal punch bag.'

I nod slowly, imagining what that must be like. I have nothing to reference it to. It's beyond my remit even to comprehend that kind of fear and pain.

'I'm sorry,' I say again.

'Yeah.' He nods, too. 'Anyway...'

'So you guys started seeing each other?'

He winced. 'I proposed to her a week after we met. I'm not good at the whole dating thing. I don't have the patience for it.' His smile is shaded with self-deprecation. 'I steamrollered her rather than dated her.'

I can't help the soft laugh that escapes me. 'Why does that not surprise me?'

It's further proof that when Jack wants something he goes after it—immediately and unequivocally. But it's taken him two years to realise he wants my body, and there's no sign he wants more than that. He felt the same love for Lucy that my grandma describes having for Grandpa. So perhaps it is normal and common and I just don't realise that because I've never felt anything like it.

It's pretty obvious Jack doesn't feel it for me. Jealousy bubbles in my gut.

'I wanted to make her life better. I wanted to fix it all. To take away her pain and make her smile and laugh.'

'I'm sure you did,' I say, with truth.

I've only seen a few photos of Lucy around the mansion and, yes, on the internet, when I've allowed myself the morbid indulgence of looking her up. And in all of these pictures she is smiling.

'I killed her, Gemma.' His eyes meet mine for a second and then he looks away. 'If she'd never met me she'd probably still be alive.'

I freeze, ill-equipped to deal with this kind of confession. Nothing about it makes sense. And yet the way he drinks after he's slept with someone... Is it possible there's a darker truth at play? No. I know Jack. I know him through and through. He's being dramatic, not literal.

'What are you talking about?'

He swallows, then closes his eyes. 'She was pregnant. We'd just found out and then the tests showed that she had cancer. I wanted her to start treatment immediately, but it would have meant her having an abortion.'

Sadness for Jack, for Lucy and for the baby they would have had fills me all the way to the top of my soul. I don't consider myself maternal, but I know instantly what decision she made and why.

'She didn't want to do that.'

'No.' His face is grim. 'Even with treatment she had pretty much no hope.' He clears his throat. 'But still... There would have been a chance. If she hadn't fallen pregnant.' He shakes his head angrily.

'Then she wouldn't have found out about the cancer until it was too late,' I say softly.

Sympathy makes me crumble. How can I be strong in the face of his loss? I cup his face and draw him to me, kissing him gently, tenderly, hoping to reassure him and wipe away this baseless and yet unending guilt.

He is still. Not kissing me back. His guilt is still cloaked about us, but then something clicks into gear and he groans into my mouth, cupping my butt and lifting my legs to wrap them around his waist, holding me against his arousal and letting me obliterate his sadness. For one more moment. One more night.

I see now that this is how he's getting through.

A night here and there to stop feeling this weight of responsibility.

A different woman to bury himself in and forget that he got Lucy pregnant and that because of her pregnancy she refused treatment.

His words swirl through my head. *I wanted to make her life better. I wanted to fix it all. To take away her pain and make her smile and laugh.*

It's exactly how I feel about Jack.

And I know one sure-fire way to bring him back from the haunted brink of the misery he's inhabiting. I kiss him hard, moving my mouth over his as I press against his cock. My hands tuck into the elastic of his swim shorts, curving around his arse, holding him tight against me.

He knows. He knows which way salvation lies and he powers through the water, walking easily to the edge and lifting me so that I'm sitting on the coping. He barely breaks our kiss as he climbs out, pressing his body over mine, his weight and wetness making me writhe against the tiles as need explodes in me.

It's the need to remove this burden from his mind, sure. But it's my own need, too. My need to *feel* him. This is what makes sense right now.

'You are like an angel,' he mutters, stripping my swimsuit from my body. The fabric is wet and stubborn, but his hands are strong and determined and dispose of it easily, rolling it down my flesh, my legs, until I can kick it off my feet. He brings his mouth back to mine and I kiss him once more, my hands grabbing his cock and guiding him towards me.

He pauses, though, his eyes seeking mine as though he's asking me something, needing something else.

I smile at him—a slow-spreading smile—and I whisper, 'Please…'

He moves inside me and something is shifting around us—changing—as tangible as the pleasure that rolls through me.

We want this to be clear-cut, yet it no longer feels that way. It's not just sex this time… It's a slow exploration that curls my toes and, I'm afraid, shakes my heart to life.

CHAPTER NINE

'I LOVE THIS CITY.'

His eyes meet mine, his smile disarming, and my body responds. I swear my breasts grin at him. Happiness settles around my shoulders.

'It's beautiful.'

A pizza box sits between us, the contents half-eaten. He reaches for another piece and I watch his fingers curl over the crust.

Making love by the pool broke something inside me and I'm glad—because it's rebuilt me in a different way. *I'm* different. *He's* different. Nothing is the same now.

'It's clean. New.' He smiles. 'Nothing like where I grew up.'

I have to shake myself into the conversation. I'm genuinely interested in where this is going, but the cobwebs of lust are hard to ignore.

'Dublin?'

'Yeah. Just outside it, anyway. A grimy little town to the east.' He wrinkles his nose.

'Do you ever get back?'

'Nah.' He throws the crust back into the box and stands up, holding his hands out to me.

I stand and put my hands in his. When did I stop questioning him and just become a part of him? And why doesn't it bother me more?

'My parents moved to Kerry—a little house overlooking the ocean, as far as you can see. It's beautiful there.'

'But you like cities?' I say as he pulls me towards him and holds me close.

He begins to sway, dancing with me on the balcony of his apartment as the moon casts a silver light over the Sydney Opera House.

'I like the pace,' he agrees. 'I'm not one for small towns.'

I tilt my head to the side. 'I don't know…' I say thoughtfully. 'I think cities can be almost slower than towns. It just depends on how you spend your time. There's certainly a lot of anonymity in a city. Haven't you ever just wanted to get lost? You can walk down Oxford Street on Boxing Day and not be seen by anyone.'

He presses his cheek against mine. There it is again. That clicking inside me as I acknowledge how right this feels. I know it's a very dangerous thought—one that will certainly lead me to pain.

'I can honestly tell you I have *never* contemplated walking down Oxford Street—let alone on Boxing Day. Are you fucking mad?'

I smile against his chest. 'Yes, well, I suppose you'd send someone to get whatever the hell you need, right?'

His smile indicates agreement.

'Anyway, you live in Hampstead. That's basically as small town as it's possible to get inside London.'

'But so close to everything. And might I point out that you live there, too?'

'I moved to Hampstead because *you* live there,' I say sensibly, and then stop moving, looking up at him with obvious embarrassment. 'Because my *job* is there,' I correct, but my cheeks are pink and my eyes can't quite meet his. 'You know…with the long hours it just made sense.'

'I know what you meant,' he says, his smile sending fire through my body. 'Where did you live before that?'

I let my breath out slowly, glad he's giving me a pass. 'Elephant and Castle.'

He laughs—a gravelled sound. 'Your parents must have *loved* that!'

They hated it. His insight shakes me. 'Why do you say that?'

'You had three nannies growing up, and a tree house big enough to sleep in. My guess would be they felt it was a bit of a fall from grace for you.'

I hide my smile by dipping my head forward. He lifts my hand and twirls me in his arms, as though we are dancing to a song that only he can hear.

'It wasn't their idea of sensible, no. But it was easy to get into work from there, and I had good friends in the area. Plus, I loved spending my Saturday mornings at Borough Market and it was an easy walk.'

'A closet foodie?' he prompts.

'No. I'm too busy to cook. But I'm a sucker for fresh flowers.' I exhale. 'And cheese. I would go from stall to stall buying whichever cheese took my fancy, savouring it that afternoon with a matched glass of wine.'

'Sounds pretty damned good.' He grins.

'Yep.'

'And you gave all that up to work for *me*, huh?'

'Not all of it,' I say with a wink. 'There's a pretty amazing cheese shop on the high street, you know.'

'And flowers?'

'Always.' I tilt my head up to his and then immediately look past him, to the glittering view of Sydney by night. There is something in his face that calls to me, and I know it would be foolish to answer it.

'Let me guess. You like white Oriental lilies?'

I'm surprised that he even knows a variety of flower, let alone is hazarding a guess as to which would be my favourite.

'No.' I shake my head. 'I love peonies and ranunculus. There's something so wildly chaotic about them that it makes my heart sing.'

'So poetic!' he teases, curling me against him and holding me tight.

I can feel his hard edges and planes, so familiar to me, but my heart is racing as though it's the first time we've touched.

'I think they're naughty,' I say with a grin. 'As though someone has said to them, *"We're going to make you the most beautiful, chubby little flowers in the world, but only if you grow straight up towards the sky."* And then they looked at each other and said, *"Nah."* Have you ever really paid attention to their stems? The way they wind round and round as though they're dancing in a thunderstorm?'

His smile is mysterious. Enigmatic. He is, at times, impossible to read.

'No.'

'No? You don't agree?'

'No, I've never looked at their stems to the degree you have. Nor have I anthropomorphised them.'

'Then you've led a very deprived life, sir.'

I feel his laugh rather than hear it: a rumble from deep in his body. 'Apparently. Do you want some dessert?'

'I can think of other things I want more.'

He laughs and shakes his head, stepping away from me and disappearing.

Thwarted desire flames at the soles of my feet.

He returns a moment later, two coffee cups in his hands. Except there's no coffee in them. They're filled with a single scoop of vanilla ice cream each.

It's sweet, but truly dessert is the last thing on my mind. Before I can tell him that he pulls a hand from behind his back and holds out two perfect fresh cherries.

I grin as he places one in each cup.

'The cherry on top,' he explains unnecessarily, and my heart turns over in my chest at this gesture that is at once both sexy and sweet. Sexy, because how can I *ever* see a cherry as just a cherry again? And sweet because it is *our* thing.

We have *a thing*.

He digs a spoon into the ice cream and brings it to my lips. I taste it, but as on that first night, with our first kiss, his mouth is on mine immediately, his tongue tasting me even as I taste the ice cream.

Dessert is forgotten.

His kiss is unlike anything I've felt with him. It's soft. Tender. Gentle.

He breathes in as though he's inhaling me and I do the same, smiling against his lips.

Despite everything we've shared, it feels like the most intimate we've ever been. As if we're connected on every level.

But then our desperate hunger takes over and his hands are pushing at my robe, connecting with my naked flesh with the same intensity that marked our first coming together. It's as though he's punishing himself now—punishing himself for wanting me in any way other than animalistic and wild.

He presses me back, his kiss hard against my face, his body firm against mine, until I connect with the glass balustrade that runs along the edge of the terrace. He drops his kiss lower, to my neck, and lower still, his stubble grazing along my front until he brushes a nipple, taking it into his mouth and sucking it, spinning whirls of pleasure through me.

He drops lower, and finally falls to his knees. His mouth against my clit is a welcome invasion, his tongue what I have been needing. I grip the railing, my hands tight around its edge, as he glides his tongue down and I moan, pressing deeper against him. He knows exactly what I like now, and it takes him only moments to stir me to a fever pitch of awareness.

I make a small sound in the night air, tilting my head back and staring up at the stars above Sydney as I fall apart against his mouth, my orgasm spellbinding in its intensity and strength. I sway, and almost fall forward, but his strong hands are gripping my hips, pulling me to him as he stands.

'You are beautiful,' he murmurs, pressing a kiss to my forehead.

My breath is burning hard in my lungs, supercharging my body. Everything about this moment is just that: beautiful.

I meet his eyes and—ridiculously—feel a stinging in the back of mine. *Don't let me cry!* How embarrassing. But there's something in his look that's spinning my gut, shifting through me with a sense of unreality. As though he's thinking something and doesn't know how to say it.

I watch him, waiting for my breath to settle and my pulse to slow. He opens his mouth. My heart is still. Then, with one of those rakish smiles I've come to love, he says, 'Let's go to bed.'

'So you're his other half? Professionally speaking.'

I smile at Clint Sheridan but my eyes are glued to Jack. Across the room he holds court easily, and a group of men and two women stand hanging on his every word.

'Technically, I'm his in-house counsel,' I say, with a sideways smile.

'But word has it that you pretty much oversee his entire workload.'

'Really?' I arch a brow and sip my champagne. 'His workload is pretty immense.'

'I can imagine.'

I like Clint. Given that he's going to be running the Australian operation, I'll have to work closely with him—certainly in the start-up phase. He's a bit nervous, but I think once he settles down into the role he'll be funny and fast. He's definitely relaxed a little, even over the course of the few hours we've been at his expansive apartment on Sydney's North Shore.

The view is spectacular—different to that from Jack's penthouse—and by night the city shimmers before us. The famed Harbour Bridge has been lit red, for some reason, and there's something almost eerie about the way it seems to glide over the water, an angry sentinel or a protective beacon. In the far distance there's a flash of lightning, and that only adds to the spectacle.

'Night show!'

Clint grins, as if following my gaze. Or perhaps he's seen the involuntary shudder—a response to the suggestion of thunder. I don't give in to temptation and ask if a storm is forecast. I'm not a little girl any more. I can recognise my phobia as just that—an illogical pattern of fear.

'Have you lived here long?' I ask.

'A few years.' He rests his hand on the back of a dark timber chair and sips his beer. 'Bought it off the plan. Thought I'd use it as a renter, but then—divorce.' He grimaces, as if the single word should communicate his entire backstory.

'I'm sorry. I didn't know.'

'Why would you?'

His smile is disarming. He's handsome, I realise. Strange that I didn't notice sooner. *Oh, yeah?* My brain is rolling its eyes again. It has a point. Finding another man attractive when I'm sleeping with Jack Grant is like taking a shower in the middle of the Niagara Falls. But there's no denying it. Clint has got eyes that are almost as dark as night, a thick crop of black hair, a swarthy tanned complexion—and he's built like a tank. Thick neck, muscled arms—like he'd be as at home on a rugby field as he would the boardroom.

Mmm.

'True. It's not really our concern if you're married or not.'

'Are you?'

My eyes lift to his, my smile hinting at a laugh. 'Definitely not.'

'That's funny?'

His eyes scan my face and there's curiosity there. I suppose I am of an age where women are generally on that path somewhere. Either dating, engaged, planning the wedding, married, just married, sick of marriage… I'm none of those things. In fact, marriage really hasn't entered my head as a desirable state into which to enter.

Out of nowhere, the wedding anniversary party fizzes into my mind. I could definitely attribute my lack of faith in the whole institution of marriage to my parents. The silence of my childhood sits like a dull weight on my periphery.

'Only in that I barely have time to plan a holiday, let alone something as monumental as—' I wave my hand in the air and the gold bangles I'm wearing jangle '—that.'

'Smart move. The whole thing's overrated.'

I arch a brow, sipping my champagne. My eyes travel across the room distractedly. They're just skimming faces and people, travelling out of habit rather than on any specific quest. But they glance across at Jack and meet his eyes and everything inside me lurches almost painfully. A primal ache of possession unfurls in my gut.

With effort, I turn my attention back to Clint. 'I suppose it's easy to feel that when you've just come out of a divorce.'

'Should never have got married,' he says with a shrug of his shoulders. 'Taught me a valuable lesson, though.'

'And what's that?'

'Gemma?'

I tilt my head, my eyes locking with Jack's once more. He's right beside me, his face unreadable.

'Am I interrupting?'

'I've never understood why people ask that. You obviously *are* interrupting.' I soften the words with a smile, but Clint tenses beside me.

'Then by all means continue,' Jack invites, his eyes challenging me silently.

'Clint was just telling me why marriage is a huge mistake.'

I turn my body away from Jack, giving Clint my full attention. Only I've made a crucial error. Jack's right behind me, and my back is completely hidden from the room. His hand curls around my arse and I have to bite my tongue to stop myself drawing in a sharp breath.

His fingers stroke my flesh, and even I can feel his warmth through the dress.

My knees are shaking suddenly.

'For me it was,' Clint backpedals, his smile dismissive.

'Sorry to hear that,' Jack says, pressing his fingers in a little deeper, shooting arrows of desire through my flesh. 'I need Gemma for a conference call I'm expecting. Is there somewhere private we can go?'

My heart is racing, beating so hard I'm surprised it can stay lodged in my chest.

'Yeah, of course—my office.' Clint nods, turning on his heel and moving through the lounge area.

Jack runs his hand higher up my back and then drops it to his side as he moves to follow Clint through the luxurious apartment. Three doors down a long, well-lit corridor, Clint pauses, his smile professional.

It's clear he has no clue how Jack's been touching me, nor what Jack and I want.

'Make yourselves at home,' he invites. 'Need water? Coffee? Anything?'

Jack shakes his head and Clint leaves, pulling the door shut behind him. The office is large, and offers another view of the harbour. There's a desk in the middle, a sofa pushed hard to the wall and a bookshelf that holds a coffee machine and a bar fridge.

My inspection is cut short by Jack.

His lips find mine and his arms curl around my back, lifting me up and bringing me closer to him.

'What are you doing to me?' he groans into my mouth, the words both a plea and a hope.

'I don't know what you mean,' I manage to say. But his tongue is fighting mine and no further conversation is possible.

His hands find the hem of my dress, lifting it just enough for Jack to be able to cup my bare arse. He groans as his fingers connect with naked skin and he pushes his arousal towards me, his cock hard and firm. My body is desperate to feel more of him. But he grinds against me and I grip his shoulders, my body weakening at this contact that is so good I can barely think straight.

He lifts one hand to my hair. It's loose around my face and he tangles his fingers in its ends then pulls up from my scalp, his fingers holding me against his mouth. His other hand slips between my legs and finds my warm heat. He runs a finger along my seam and I whimper into his mouth, so wet and hot for him.

He pushes into me—just a finger, and just enough to make my body throb. I need something. Space. Breath. But his tongue lashes my mouth as his finger teases my insides, and pleasure is a spiral I cannot escape, cannot control. It spins in my gut, my chest, my heart, my blood.

I whimper again—a tiny noise locked in the back of my throat—and his fingers tighten in my hair. I am trapped by him, by this, our need for each other. His finger swirls, finding my most sensitive cluster of nerves, and I am shaking all over, from head to toe, my body his to please and command.

'Come for me,' he instructs into my mouth, as though he has heard my thoughts and knows I will do anything he asks of me.

My knees can barely hold me. Without Jack's support I would be a puddle of bones and haute couture on the elegant carpeted floor of Clint Sheridan's office.

Jack kisses me in a rhythm matched by his finger's invasion and I am falling apart in his arms, with no chance of reprieve or pause. No break in the assault of pleasure he is inflicting on me. He kisses me as I moan, my breath snatched, my blood fevered. And even as my muscles clamp around him, squeezing the pleasure from my body, his finger continues to tease me, so that the pleasure and awareness is almost unbearable.

The first orgasm is crashing around me even as a second, bigger one builds, and I grip his lapels, holding him as my world shatters in a mind-blowing moment of sexual awakening. I am fevered and limp, broken and whole.

But he's not done with me. Even as wave after wave of pleasure crashes across my brow his hands reach down, finding his zip and freeing his arousal. I know I have only seconds to regain my senses. To exercise my control in this situation that is eating me alive.

'No,' I say, and the word is thick with desire, fevered by need.

He stops, his eyes locked to mine, anguish clear in his expression. But he stops. Waits.

'Sit down,' I say, nodding towards the sofa.

Something like relief spreads over his face as he nods and moves to the sofa.

'Do you have a…'

He's reaching for his wallet before I can finish, fishing out a foil square. I groan as I slide it down his cock and then I am on top of him, straddling him, taking his length deep inside me, revelling in his possession and in his look of wonderment. Seeing that he is as lost to this pleasure as I am.

I move up and down his length, rocking on my haunches. His fingers dig into my sides, moving with me, but I am in control. When I feel him pump, so close to coming, I sit higher, so that only his tip is inside me, and he groans, tilting his head back as waves of pleasure engulf his being. I laugh softly, lowering myself back onto him and leaning forward, kissing his neck, his throat, tasting the desire that has overheated us both.

He holds my hips, keeping me low against him, and thrusts into me. My body is already on fire. It takes nothing for further flames to take hold, spreading like wildfire through my blood. My cry is muffled by his kiss, and he kisses me as together we explode.

Lightning flashes in the sky—closer now—but I barely notice. Even as rain begins to lash the windows I am aware only of *this*. Our own little storm, raging through our souls.

CHAPTER TEN

HE'S WATCHING ME, so I try to subdue my reaction. But as lightning and thunder burst almost simultaneously, and rain hammers the enormous windows and the roof of the pool room, I am quivering.

'You're actually terrified,' he murmurs with be-musement, his fingers brushing my shoulder as he removes the lightweight jacket I wore to Clint's.

'I'm not,' I lie, stepping away from him before he can detect the fine tremble in my body.

I dig my fingernails into my palms, staring out at the raging storm. It's furious and I can't stand it. If I was alone I would put earphones in and dig myself under my duvet to wait it out. But I can't, and he's still watching me.

My voice is scratchy when I speak. 'It was such a nice day. Where did this come from?'

'It's the tropics,' he points out, stepping out of his shoes and shrugging free of his jacket at the same time.

His jacket is slightly crumpled at the front, from where I curled my fingers into it as he drove me to multiple orgasms.

'Heat builds up, then it breaks in a storm.'

'Why does *that* sound familiar?'

His half-smile shows he agrees. We are our own tropical weather system. Sultry heat, storm clouds and flash floods without warning. And plenty of lightning and thunder, too.

A spike of lightning floods the lounge with an eerie glow and I jump. 'God!'

'It's only a storm,' he murmurs, closing the distance between us, his eyes locked to mine as his thumb presses beneath my chin, lifting my face to his, exposing me to his curiosity and inspection. 'It will pass.'

My stomach twists painfully now as the metaphor takes on new resonance. Is he trying to be cryptic? Is he talking about the surge of awareness that thunders between us? About us? Of course this will pass. What else do I expect?

'Sit with me.'

He squeezes my hand and draws me to him, holding me to his side as we cross the lounge to the white leather sofa that offers the most spectacular view of the harbour. The opera house is ghoulishly lit in white, and the rain lashing against it creates the impression of fog and apocalypse.

'Even the air smells different.' I inhale the acrid, electrical thickness of the atmosphere.

'Yeah…' The word is hoarse.

He sits, and I go to take the seat next to him, but he pulls me closer, landing me softly on his lap. And now his kiss is gentle. Soft. A kiss of reassurance that scares me all the more because of the way it shakes my heart to life.

I panic. This is too much. *Everything* is too much. I'm in the eye of two storms and I don't know if I'll survive either one of them.

'Tonight went well,' he says, his hand stroking my bare arm, comforting and confounding all at once.

'What do you think of the team?' I ask, finding what I hope will be common ground in our established business dynamic. Some reassurance from the familiarity of that life.

'Competent,' he says thoughtfully. 'I'm not sold on Ryan being a good fit.'

'What makes you say that?'

I feel him shrug, the movement brushing the crispness of his shirt against my skin.

'Instinct.'

'He comes highly recommended.'

'I know.'

He runs his hand over his chin and I hold my breath as I'm seared by the memory of him pressing his finger inside me, holding me as I fell apart. My gut clenches and my insides are slick with a swirling tempest of knowledge of what we've done.

'There's just something about him that seems wrong. I can't explain.'

I think back to the evening, trying to capture the same sense Jack has, and shake my head. 'We'll see, I suppose.'

'His contract has a three-month probation period?'

'Yes. I'll make a note to come over and review him at two months, though, if you're concerned.'

'Great.'

Lightning bursts again and I jump automatically.

He presses his forehead against my shoulder, the strangeness of the gesture not taking anything away from how reassuring I find it.

'Were your parents cross with you?'

'My parents? When?'

They'll be back in England now. I should probably go and see them. The thought cools the warmth in my body.

'The night you slept in the tree house.'

'Oh.' I shift a little, angling my body closer to his. 'Furious.' Then I shake my head. 'Actually, that's not true. They were disappointed.'

'Disappointed?'

'Disappointed that I'd not been cared for to their standards. Embarrassed that people might think they'd hired substandard domestic staff.' I grimace. 'Perhaps ashamed they hadn't thought to check on me when they got home—most parents would, after all.'

'You're not close to them?'

'Why do you say that?'

'Just the way you speak of them.'

'No. I'm *not* close to them. They're not that thrilled with my life choices.'

'Really? Graduating with a double first from Oxford isn't what they had in mind?'

'Hell, no. I was supposed to marry someone fancy and respectable, with a country estate to match but not better our own. And to appear in *Harper's Bazaar* articles…have tea at Kensington Palace.' I can't help rolling my eyes. 'I'm exhausted just *thinking* about what they wanted for me.'

'You don't strike me as someone who's into the society scene at all.'

'I'm not.' I shake my head. 'Their wedding anniversary is in a week, and it'll be a who's who of the British aristocracy. And, yes, *Harper's Bazaar* will be there.'

'You don't want to go?'

'I *have* to go,' I say. 'It's just—'

Thunder rolls around the apartment and I swear the windows shake in their frames. *We're going to die.*

He holds me tighter. 'It's just…?'

I don't know if he's trying to distract me from the storm or if he's really interested in my dysfunctional family, but talking *is* distracting me and distractions are good. Besides which, having opened up to him, I'm not finding it easy to curtail my thoughts.

'I'm always trotted out as proof of their happiness. Their marriage is a success. They've had a child. An heiress. I swear they actually *call* me their heiress during their toasts every year—like that's my soul function in life. To inherit.' I shake my head. 'I *hate* that. I've hated it for as long as I have understood their expectations. Or lack thereof. My existing is sufficient for their needs. My ambitions are irrelevant and slightly offensive to them. And my working for *you* is definitely tantamount to slashing the family tapestries.'

'You make them sound like selfish bastards.'

I laugh. 'Do I?'

'*Are* they?'

His fingers are glancing over my skin, stirring warmth and desire inside my chest.

'They're products of their upbringings,' I say, and then shake my head, for it's disloyal to Grandma to implicate her in my father's cold-fishery. He's really a grump of his own creation. 'Or perhaps of society's expectations. I don't know. They're very…stiff upper lip. Cold. Emotionless.'

His lips twist. 'Funny. That's just how I would have described *you* a few weeks ago.'

My eyes widen and I look at him. 'There's a huge

difference between maintaining a professional distance and being cold.'

'Yes, there is.' His finger lifts higher, running a line over my cheek. 'You were doing both.'

'I was *not*,' I deny, offended by his description.

'You made ice look warm.'

I move to stand, but his hands still me. 'Why?' he asks. 'Why did you act like that around me?'

'It wasn't an *act*.' I sniff, staring out at the storm-ravaged harbour.

But Jack's insistent. 'You're not like it with anybody else. I never really noticed that until I saw you talking with Wolf DuChamp. And now I've paid better attention I see you weren't like it with anyone but me.'

'I...I was. That's just how I am.'

'No.' He's adamant. 'The guys from the Tokyo transition team all call you "Gem", like you're some long-lost buddy of theirs. You're friendly with Rose and Sophia. Amber raves about you. It's just me.'

I open my mouth to deny it, but how can I? He's totally right. I met Jack Grant and every single one of my defences was raised because I *knew*. I knew there was trouble on our doorstep: a chemistry we would need to work our butts off to deny.

'So what *is* it about me, Gemma Picton, that had you acting as though I were the plague incarnate?'

My heart hammers hard in my chest. There is danger in this conversation. Danger of truth and honesty and far too much insight.

'Maybe I thought you'd see friendliness as encouragement,' I murmur, my tone light, going for a joke.

'But not with Wolf or Barry or Clint?'

My expression is calm, but inside I'm shivering. 'No.' It's a whisper.

God. What is he doing to me? He seems to have become 'just Jack', but my brain reminds me forcefully that the man made a billion-pound fortune virtually from scratch. He's brilliant, ruthless and incisive. And determined.

'When did you realise this was going to happen?' He runs his finger higher, teasing my nipple through the flimsiness of my dress.

I arch a brow, my breath trapped in my throat. 'Um… around the night you kissed me and…touched me…'

It's a lie. I knew it from the moment I accepted the job. Proximity would feed inevitability. On reflection, I can't believe I stalled it for two years.

'I think you've wanted me longer than that.'

'Do you?' I clear my throat, and this time when I stand, he doesn't stop me.

I feel his eyes on my back as I walk into the kitchen and pour a glass of mineral water. The bubbles are frantic—hypnotic, even.

'Yeah.'

He stands, and I look at him helplessly.

'What do you want me to say?' I lift my shoulders. 'I knew you, Jack. I *know* you. I know that you're in love with your wife. I know that you sleep with women to forget her. Do you blame me for wanting to keep this insanity at bay?'

'No.' He drags a hand through his hair and his smile is ghostly on his face. 'I blame myself for not letting you.'

His shoulders are broad, and an invisible, enormous weight is upon them.

'I blame myself for not being strong, like you were. You wanted me, but you were never going to do a damned thing about it—were you?'

'Of course not. Apart from anything else, you're my boss. And that's *before* I think about the steady stream of women filing through your bedroom. This is probably the dumbest thing I've ever done.'

'Yes.' He nods, his eyes locked to mine. 'But you don't want it to end.'

I shake my head, seeking refuge in honesty at last. 'Do *you*?'

'No.' And now his smile is broader. 'Turns out I'm scared of something else.'

'What's that?'

'How much I want you. Need you. And I'm scared of hurting you, Gemma.'

'You won't.'

He nods, but I know he's not convinced. Nor am I. In fact, I would say Jack hurting me is as inevitable as the morning that will break over the harbour in the next few hours. But I don't care. Having given in to this, I am just a tree in the middle of a storm, trying my hardest to hold on, to stand tall even as it threatens to uproot me for good.

The mood is oppressive. Suddenly I want to lighten it. To make him smile. To feel his warmth and contentment.

'I bet you were a real little shit growing up.'

The ghost of our conversation lingers, but he makes a visible effort to push it away. 'Why do you say that?'

'Hmm...remember who you're talking to? You're stubborn and selfish...'

'Selfish, huh? I always look after *you*...'

My face burns hot and I'm sure it's flame-red. 'I didn't mean in bed,' I mumble.

His laugh is my reward. Sweet and husky, it makes my nerves quiver.

'I see…'

Perhaps he takes pity on me. He strides across the kitchen and props his arse against the kitchen counter. I imagine his tattoo through the tailored cut of his trousers and absent-mindedly slide my hand out and curve it over his hip.

'I was a good kid, actually,' he says, not reacting to my touch visibly.

I like the intimacy of this, though. Perhaps more than I should. Of being able to reach out and feel him, to sense his nearness.

'So your recalcitrance came later in life?'

He laughs. 'I guess so.'

His hand lifts and wraps around my cheek. I inhale. This moment, his fragrance—everything. I fold the memory away and store it for later delight. It is a perfect slice of time.

'I went away to school.'

'A boarding school?'

His nod is a small movement—just a jerk of his head. 'I won a full scholarship.'

'And you call *me* an overachiever?' I tease.

His smile is indulgent. 'I had no choice. There was only one way out of the backwater I grew up in. I succeeded because the prospect of failure was too depressing to contemplate. You, on the other hand, m'lady, are motivated by something I don't understand. You had everything… You were born with a fortune and a family lineage that dates back to the Magna Carta…

It would have been so easy for you to stay within the boundaries of that life. And it would have been a *good* life.'

'It depends on how you define "good",' I say simply. 'I've never fitted in.'

'I find that impossible to believe.'

'Why?'

'You could fit in anywhere.'

'Trust me—I didn't want to feel at home in *that* crowd.'

His frown is just a very slight twist of his lips. 'So your parents are stuffy. What about your friends?'

'Most of my closest friends I met later. At university. Then at Goldman. Deloitte.'

'And here? With me?'

For a second my heart skids to a stop, because I think he's talking about himself and there is something so delightfully needy about the question that I ache for him.

But then he continues. 'Wolf. Barry. You seem to know everyone who works for me.'

'Oh, right...' Emptiness is a gulf in the pit of my stomach. 'That happens. *Your* parents must be proud of *you*.' I shift the conversation to him, hating the vulnerabilities he's able to expose in me so easily.

'Yes.'

He moves a little, bringing his body closer to mine, and then, before I know what he's doing, he lifts me onto the bench, spreading my legs and standing between them.

He's so close I'm sure he must be able to hear the thundering of my heart; it is surpassed only by the storm outside.

'My parents thought I would—at most—become an accountant. Like my father and his father before him. I was always good at numbers. It fair skittled them when I told them I'd bought my first company.'

'Yeah, I can see how that would bowl them over.'

His laugh is husky. He brushes his lips against the soft skin at the base of my throat, chasing the wildly beating pulse-point with his tongue. I moan, deep in my mouth, the sound strangled by my own hot, thick breath.

'You make it sound easy. Like you didn't want to be an accountant so you did this instead.'

'This?' He laughs, flicking the strap of my dress so it falls haphazardly down my arm, revealing my shoulder to him.

His kiss is sweet, like nectar. He finds the exposed skin and possesses it as only Jack Grant can, gliding his mouth over it, making me feel I have never before been kissed. It is at once intimate and simple and my back arches forward. Or backwards. Who can tell? The normal rules of gravity and physics seem not to apply.

'How do you know my family dates back to the Magna Carta?' I ask, though the words are squeezed tight from my chest, not quite coming out clearly.

But he hears. He understands. 'I looked you up,' he says unapologetically.

'You…?'

His mouth drops lower and at the same time he lifts my hand, drags the kiss to my inner wrist. I squeeze my eyes shut as he finds another pulse-point, tracing it with his tongue.

'I searched you on the internet,' he confirms, dropping my hand gently and cupping my arse, pulling me closer to him.

I wrap my legs around his waist. 'Why?'

'Because you surprised me the other night. I realised I should have known this stuff.'

'What stuff?'

'All of it. Your dynastic birthright.'

I laugh.

'What's funny?'

'Just… Only *you* would want to know more and decide to look it up rather than ask.'

'Asking would have taken time,' he says with an unapologetic lift of his broad strong shoulders.

'And we don't have time?'

'I'm impatient.' He grins.

'I had no idea.' Sarcasm is rich in my murmured tone.

His hands are on my knees and then they're tracing higher, his fingertips barely brushing my flesh as he searches for the softness of my inner thighs.

'Is that weird?'

I pause, concentration almost impossible. 'Is *what* weird?'

His lips are buzzing mine, just the smallest hint of contact making every nerve ending in my body sing. 'That I ran an internet search on you.'

'Oh.' I frown. 'It should be. But, no. For you it makes sense.'

His laugh is breathed across my skin, sending it into a break-out of goose bumps.

'Because I'm weird?'

'Because you're *you*,' I correct. 'Domineering, determined, somewhat wonderful you.'

He's still for a moment. Frozen by the compliment he didn't expect. Then he relaxes again, his lips are on my skin and my heart is flying out of my body, soaring above me. This is so *right*. So *perfect*. Out of nowhere I am in heaven.

'Are you saying you haven't done a search on me?' he teases, his hands lifting to the zip at the back of my dress and catching it lower, snagging it over my spine. My body is hypersensitive; I feel every single kink of his touch.

I have. I've looked him up *and* his wife. Something I am naturally hesitant to confess.

'I applied to work for you,' I say with a shrug. 'Of course I did.'

His laugh shows he knows me to be lying. Or at least being liberal with the truth.

'Why did you move your office from the City?' The question is blurted out of me before I even realise I've been wondering.

He pauses, the zip halfway down my back, his mouth so close to mine I want to push up and find him. But he's still, and the question hangs between us, and I realise I do want to hear the answer.

'Sorry?'

'I just… Speaking of questions…' My throat thumps as I swallow. 'Is it because of Lucy?'

His expression flashes with something. Anguish?

I shake my head quickly. 'Forget it. I shouldn't have asked.'

'No.' It's a gravelled denial. 'It's fine.'

But I might as well have lashed him with a stick dipped in lava.

'It *was* because of Lucy. She was sick at the end.

I set my home up so I could be near her all the time. The room…the bedroom near my office… That was her room.'

Oh, God. How did I not know that? His little 'den of sin' held his dying wife's sickbed.

A shudder rips through me as the macabre sadness of it all washes over me.

'After she died I just… I didn't want life to go back to normal. I resented the implication that it would.'

He expels an angry sigh and now his fingers are pushing my zip down almost dispassionately.

'There's no textbook on grief.'

'Of course there's not.'

'But I expected to cope better than I did.'

His eyes sweep shut. He's shielding himself from me, but at least he keeps talking. That's enough. It *has* to be enough.

'We had months to prepare. To brace ourselves. She was ready. Her life at the end was…' He changes direction, as though he's somehow betraying Lucy. 'She was ready to go. My therapist tells me I spent so long being strong for Lucy that I had nothing left to give myself.'

'You have a therapist?'

'I did. Until he spouted *that* piece of pretty bullshit. As if there's a finite amount of support to give. As if I should have ignored Lucy's needs in favour of my own.'

'I don't think he meant that. Lucy's sickness must have been draining on you. I can imagine that you spent so much of your energy focussing on what she needed that you had no idea what to do with yourself once she passed.'

'It shook my world,' he said simply.

I'm so sorry for him. But I don't say that because

I've said it before. My dress is loose around my waist.
I'm not wearing a bra and his hands run up my sides
and cup my breasts as though holding them is his only
form of salvation.

'It still does,' I say softly.

'It's different now.'

He runs his thumb over my nipple, his eyes drawn
downwards, his attention focussed on the physicality
of my body, rather than me.

'Different how?' I need to know. I want to understand.

'I grieve for her, but I can function. The hardest days
aren't the ones that fill me with sadness.'

'No?'

'No, Gemma.'

He lifts me up, off the bench, wrapping me around
him as he walks through the apartment, towards his
bedroom. But I don't want him to close this conversation down.

'What are the hardest days?' I push as he shoulders
the door inwards.

He lays me down on the bed and I scramble into a
sitting position, not caring that my dress is simply a belt
at my hips and my body is exposed to him completely.

'Days like this. Days when I am happy and distracted. Days when I forget to remember her. The worst
days now are the days when I realise I haven't thought
of her at all. Days like today, when all I've had room
for on my mind is *you*.'

My heart turns over and, God, I am the worst kind
of human because I delight in his admittance even as
I realise I am triumphing over a dead woman.

Telling myself Lucy would want him to be happy,

I stand up onto the tips of my toes so I can kiss him, and then pull him backwards onto the bed.

'Being happy doesn't mean you loved her any less,' I promise him softly as I flick his buttons open and run my fingertips over his chest. 'It just means you're human and that time is moving on. It's normal. It's natural.'

He doesn't answer, but his kiss is all the response I need. It is sweet and it is gentle and it is a promise from his body that I know he's not yet ready to make with his words.

The first week Gemma came to work for me I pushed her like a demon. I was so sick of the string of quitters before her that I'd developed a foolproof way to flush them out. I started them at six o'clock each morning, demanding different sets of information in advance and then what I actually required. This was to see how they thought on their feet.

She was amazing.

When she didn't have a ready answer she would procure it easily and without fuss. She was honest about what she didn't know and she stared me down when I tried to imply that her inefficiencies were a result of a flaw in her preparation.

She worked late, travelled to Paris with me on a minute's notice and never once complained.

And then one day I went into her office and found her asleep, just like she is now. Her head dropped on the desk, her hair like golden silk across her keyboard.

That was the first time I told myself she was off-limits. I wanted her even then. My body responded instantly, and in my mind I fantasised about acting on my desire. Making her mine. But it would have been a transient pleasure. And even then, when I hardly knew her, I knew she was a rare, fascinating object—someone I could never touch. Never hurt.

Yet here I am.

Here *she* is.

At some point during the night, after I'd fallen asleep, Gemma must have stirred and taken herself back to her room, respecting those unspoken boundaries we've erected even after I told her more about myself than I ever have another soul.

And that angers me. It angers me that she accepts those limitations even now.

It is not yet dawn, but the sky is glistening with the promise of morning and a hint of golden light steals through the blinds, marking her cheek and her arm. I wonder what it would be like to lift the cover and lie beside her. To wrap her to my chest and kiss her awake softly. To stir her body with mine.

But the day is breaking, and she is just as off-limits to me now as she was two years ago.

CHAPTER ELEVEN

My plane lands at seven. How soon can you be at my place?

I SMILE AT the text but my heart sinks. A week after I returned from Australia and Jack is almost home. A problem with the winery in New Zealand required his urgent personal attention, and as a result I have been in sexual purgatory for seven days and nights.

I am aching for him physically and, yes, I miss him. I miss him so much I can no longer doubt just what form my feelings take.

I love him.

I am in love with him.

And, just like Grandma described, it has hit me out of nowhere. It is a realisation and it is also an incontrovertible law of nature now, as unquestionable and rock-solid as gravity, helium, oxygen and rain.

I run a hand down my pale green sheath dress, feeling its silkiness and wishing like hell it was his hands, not mine, on my body.

Tomorrow morning…?

I wait for a moment, but he doesn't reply. Jack has Wi-Fi enabled on his jet, and he's always in contact, so I don't doubt he's got the message. I imagine his lips drawing down at the corners as he contemplates the fact that I'm not simply fitting in with what he's suggested.

By 'tomorrow morning' do you mean 7.05 p.m.?

I laugh and shake my head, reaching for my bronzer and giving my face one last flush of colour. My make-up is exquisite—I didn't do it, so I can say that. My hair has been styled into a rather vintage crimp, and a diamond clip is tethered just above one ear, adding to the *Great Gatsby* look.

I grab a stole and slip into my shoes, then scoop up my phone.

I wish. It's my parents' anniversary party, remember?

I thrust the phone into my bag and press it beneath my arm.

My driver is waiting. Not Hughes. *My* driver. The one I use when I have family stuff on and Mum and Dad like to know I'm observing the little rituals that matter to them. Like being chauffeured.

'Hey...' I smile distractedly, sliding into the back seat. I look at my phone.

Shit. I forgot. Skip it?

I laugh.

I wish.

What are you wearing?

I grin, lift the phone up and take a shot of myself. I examine it quickly—one chin, eyes open, passably attractive—and then send it to him.

His response is almost immediate.

Smoking hot, Lady Gemma.

My heart turns over in my chest and for a mini-second I contemplate blowing the party off—to hell with the consequences—and going to Jack instead. My parents would be furious, but I suspect it would be worth it...

I text him back.

What are YOU wearing?

A few seconds later I am rewarded with a photo of him. I stare at the screen and my heart thumps hard in my chest. He is gorgeous. So beautiful. So danger-ously, darkly, distractingly beautiful.

I stare at his eyes and feel as though I really am looking at him.

You're flying in a SUIT? What happened to comfort?

He doesn't respond immediately and I put my phone into my bag, letting my eyes catch up with the passing scenery. The anniversary celebration is to be at The Ritz—where else?—and the car eats up the distance from Hampstead into the West End, skirting Kensington Gardens on one side.

I check my phone again as we pull to a stop—nothing.

Disappointment fills me, but I will see him soon. Tomorrow. And we'll make up for lost time.

Just looking at that photo is enough to get me off. But I need more than that. I need to be held by him. To feel his arms wrapping around me, to look up at him and know that his heart is beating for mine…

'Madam.' The driver opens the door and I smile at him, stepping out into the cool night air.

Flashes go off in my face. I'm unprepared. Foolishly, really, given the high-profile nature of the party and the venue that's designed to draw attention. I just haven't been focussing on it at all. I plaster a smile on my face as I dip my head forward and clip towards the large glass doors.

The party is in The Music Room. I've been there once before, for my grandfather's birthday, I remember as I step over the threshold. The room is the very definition of elegance, with gold and pink highlights, enormous floral arrangements and curtains that look like they weigh a tonne.

I'm late. Only ten minutes or so, but the room is full. The music is a perfectly refined string quartet, and my parents are at the end of a receiving line, like a scene from a Jane Austen book.

I pause, wondering if I can sneak away before they see me, go and find Grandma. I'd put money on her being near the bar…

But my mother's eyes meet mine and her hand lifts, waving me over.

I swear under my breath, plastering a smile on my face. 'Mum.' I kiss her cheek. 'You look lovely.'

She does. Mum is always stunning. And now, after her jaunting about—rather, her international philanthropy—she's acquired a caramel tan. Her outfit is almost bridal—a cream lace prom dress that falls to just below her knees. Dad is in a tux.

'Welcome home,' I say.

'Oh, yes. That's right. We haven't seen you since we got back.' Her lips pucker in disapproval.

'I've been in Australia,' I explain awkwardly, then wish I hadn't. Why the heck am I apologising? It's not like they've been tripping over themselves to organise a reunion. 'Was it a good trip?'

My father grumbles something I don't quite catch.

'Quite.' Mother nods. 'We're thinking of going again next year—aren't we, darling?'

His look is one of long-suffering tolerance. 'We'll see.'

'Is Grandma here?'

My mother nods, her eyes flitting across the room. 'In that direction.'

'I'll go and check on her,' I say, as though it's a service I can offer when in fact I am serving only myself.

'Is your speech ready, darling?' Mother calls to me as I leave.

I wince. *Shit.* Why didn't I remember I'd have to do a speech?

I cut through the crowd until my eyes land on Grandma. Her wiry figure is perfectly framed by a jet-black dress and a bolero that has a fine silver thread to it. She's wearing dark silk flowers at the collar and she manages to look rather funereal.

I laugh as I approach. 'Hey!'

'Oh, thank fuck. Someone I actually *like*.'

Several people hear her curse and move away disapprovingly. I grin, kissing her papery cheek.

'Tell me about it... I think this is an even duller crowd than usual.' I tap the bar, my eyes catching the bartender's. 'Champagne.'

He pours a glass of Bollinger and hands it to me. Grandma signals for a top-up and I wonder, with a disguised smile, how many glasses she's already knocked back. She can hold her liquor like a sailor, and age isn't slowing that down.

'Where's my koala?'

'Your...huh?'

'You went to Australia, didn't you?' she asks impatiently.

'Oh. Yeah, right. Guess what? Turns out you *do* have to go bush to see one.'

'And let me guess? You were working too hard for that?'

'Mmm...'

It wasn't all work. My body flushes with remembered pleasure. Jack's touch was worth travelling to the other side of the world for.

'I did see dolphins from Jack's balcony, though. They were amazing. A whole pod of them, just gliding and...frolicking.'

'They were on the balcony?'

'No, Grandma, they were in the harbour.' I laugh.

'Obviously, dear.' She takes another sip of champagne. 'Remember your grandfather's birthday?'

I nod. 'I was thinking of it when I came in.'

'He was so happy that night. To be surrounded by

his loved ones.' She sighs, her eyes a little watery as she looks around the room. 'The mayor's here.'

I follow her gaze. 'Yes. Dad and he have been doing some work together, I think.'

Grandma's brows lift skyward, as if imbuing even that with a response of disapproval. I sip my champagne.

'You had a good time, then?'

'Yeah. Australia's beautiful. I like Sydney.'

'So why did you come back?'

I laugh. 'You're turning into a one-track record.'

'Darling, life's too short for pleasantries, and I love you too much to lie.'

'I live *here*. I'd miss *you*, apart from anything.'

'I'd come and visit.'

We're interrupted by an old friend of my father's, and for the next twenty minutes Grandma and I make polite conversation, all the while subtly—and, I fear, not so subtly—nudging one another's ankles and trying not to roll our eyes.

There is someone else after that, and then my grandma's goddaughter Laurena—another story altogether...*ugh!* And then, before I know it, it's half past seven.

Jack will have landed by now. In his suit. So handsome; such a waste.

I sigh and refocus my attention on the conversation I'm half involved in, nodding as required, and then I'm actually grateful when my father asks me to dance with him. There's only a small makeshift dance floor—a concession to the fact that there are so many guests and most of them are not interested in dancing.

But Dad and I have always danced. He wraps his arms around me and it reminds me of when I was a little girl, standing on his feet, moving in time to the music. And it's a hell of a lot better than shooting the breeze with my parents' friends.

I feel a wave of sympathy for Grandma, whom I have deserted and left to the well-heeled wolves. I look over my shoulder to see her holding court and wonder, with a distracted smile, what she's talking about.

'How's work, pumpkin?'

I blink back to my father. 'Great.'

'Really? That's a shame.'

'It is?'

'Sidney was just saying he could use a consultant with your skill set.'

'Mayor Black?' I prompt, my smile wry.

'He's admired your career for a long time. Asked if I'd set up a meeting.'

'I've got a job, Daddy. A job I love.'

And then, as if I have somehow conjured him from my longing and imagination, Jack is beside us, his eyes intense as they lock solely to mine, his expression inscrutable. It is him and me—*us*. Just us.

'Jack?' I stop dancing altogether and take a small step away from my dad. I can hardly catch my breath. 'What are you doing here?'

'You invited me. Remember?'

I did no such thing, and we both know it, but I'm not going to point that out in front of my father.

'Right, of course.' I nod. Blood is roaring through my veins. 'I forgot. Dad, this is Jack Grant. My...er...boss.'

Jack extends his hand and shakes my father's with his natural confidence. 'My Lord.'

My father is in awe—like most people who first meet Jack. It pleases me. For all he hates the hours I work, and the commitment I have to my job, he obviously understands the unique thrill that comes from working with someone like Jack.

'Mind if I cut in?'

'Oh, I… Of course not.'

My father steps back, but I don't see him move away because Jack wraps his arms around me and consumes all my senses.

He overpowers me with his nearness and his uniqueness. He moves in time to the music but I feel his body, tight and hard, and my gut clenches.

'What are you really doing here?'

There is something I don't understand in his features. A haunted expression. Anger?

'You seem kind of uptight about this. I've never seen you like that about anything.'

I nod slowly. Does he think that explains anything?

'So…?'

'I was at a loose end.'

'Oh.' My heart thumps painfully. 'Right.'

What was I expecting? Flowery declarations of love?

'You were my plan,' he says gently, his fingers running over my back. 'I wanted to see you. And you were here.'

'So you came here?' I murmur, crossing over into unnecessary repetition and not caring.

Because my heart is floating away from my body, thumping high in the sky over us.

'Pretty much.'

His smile makes my stomach flip and flop and twist and turn.

'Well, I'm not so sure I want to be here now.'

His laugh undoes the last stitch of my sanity. I want to strip my clothes off and cry out, *Take me now!*

'My evil plan.' He grins. 'How's your week been?'

Is this really happening? Is Jack Grant at my parents' wedding anniversary party, dancing with me, stroking my back, asking me about my week, telling me he's missed me? Or am I somehow dreaming this up? It doesn't make sense.

'Busy. Yours?'

Wow. I sound normal. Good job, me!

'Perfect.' He winks—so sexy. 'New Zealand is stunning; the winery is incredible.'

My sigh is wistful. 'I'll bet.'

He chuckles. 'You'll see it for yourself next time you're over.'

'Yeah…'

I try not to get too swept up in fantasies that involve Jack and me skipping down the rows of grapes, holding hands, laughing into the sunset. Fantasies are nice, but they're not real life.

'Jack Grant?'

I feel his sigh but he hides it well, turning to look at the man who's come to address us. I recognise him, but can't think of his name in that moment.

'Adam.' Jack nods, not relinquishing his grip around my waist. 'How's it going?'

'Jesus, I haven't seen you in *years*. I've kept up with you, of course. Amazing career. Got a moment? I'd love to talk to you about a project I'm in the middle of.'

'Actually…' Jack says, and my heart leaps.

But we're attracting attention, and I'm not sure either of us is ready to deal with that yet.

I clear my throat and step backwards. 'It's fine.' I

wince inwardly when I hear the ice-cold tone that bleats from my lips. I soften it with effort, stretching my lips into a smile. 'I want to go check on my grandma, anyway.'

'Ah, she's here?' Jack's eyes glint with shared knowledge. My gut somersaults. 'I look forward to meeting her.'

His gaze holds mine for a moment too long and the universe vibrates differently—just for us.

I smile as I walk away, swinging my butt, knowing that not only is he here with me tonight because he cares for me, but that soon we're going to be making love and I cannot wait.

'Things are making a little more sense now,' Grandma murmurs, her eyes trained on Jack's profile.

He's locked in conversation with the man—Adam—his expression instantly businesslike. My heart thumps.

'What do you mean?' I reach down and sip her champagne, taking the seat beside her.

Grandma taps my knee. 'It isn't just a job.'

I contemplate denial, but it's Grandma. She'll see through it.

'Meaning?' I say instead, cautious. Waiting.

'You're seeing him?'

Trust Grandma. I bite down on my lip. 'Not really. Kind of.'

'You love him?'

My heart throbs. I look at her and shake my head, but my smile tells a different story.

'I see.' She tilts her head, her eyes pinned to Jack as though she's pulling him apart, piece by piece. 'Interesting…'

'Not really.' I shake my head. 'And it's very…early. New.'

'Secret?' she supplies, her eyes flitting to mine and sparkling with the hint of mystery I've evoked. I sigh. There'll be no stopping her now.

'Yes, secret,' I say after a beat.

'Fine. I can do secret.' She winks at me and taps my knee once more.

It's more than an hour before I get near Jack again, and by then I am *desperate* to touch him. To kiss him. To be alone with him. I'm almost there—just a few people to navigate—when my parents take to the stage and the music goes silent. The guests follow suit.

My mother is a natural-born performer. She speaks easily to the crowd, playing the part of happy wife perfectly. My father toasts her and then they introduce me. Their heir.

Ugh.

I paste a smile on my face, sashaying close enough to Jack on my way to the stage that his hands brush my hip and my body charges with electricity.

I'll do the damned tribute speech and then we'll go. Him and me. Alone time with him is the talisman on the periphery of my mind.

There are a heap of people looking back at me, but I see only Jack. His eyes seem to caress me, even from this distance. A pulse throbs between my legs. Desire is a tangible force, wrapping me in its determined grip.

'I've been thinking about love and marriage a lot lately. About the leap of faith required to take that step. We can enter into a relationship with the best of intentions and find that it doesn't work out. That our love alone isn't enough—that it doesn't go the distance. Or perhaps we lose the person we love most on earth, and feel robbed of our soul mate. Our love.'

My eyes hold Jack's and I blink, my heart twisting.

'Or perhaps we fall in love and marry and everything is perfect. A true happily-ever-after.'

I turn and smile at my parents, hoping that these vague descriptions of love will somehow mean something to them. It's hard to tell. Botox has rendered my mother's range of visible reactions down to single digits. There's disapproval, impatience, wry amusement and boredom. I don't know which of these she's feeling, so I turn back to the assembled guests.

'My grandma talks about meeting my grandpa almost as if the moment was divined by fate. There was an inevitability to their life and love—one she couldn't have fought even if she'd wanted to.'

I smile at Grandma and the tears in her eyes make me proud, because she understands that I *know*. I know what she felt.

'I think marriage is a remarkable thing, and I congratulate my parents on thirty years of it. To Mum and Dad.'

I lift the glass in my hand and smile at them.

My mother nods her thanks. Dad blows me a kiss. The crowd repeats my toast and I walk off stage.

I set my champagne flute down on the edge of a table and don't look at another soul. Instead I walk towards the doors, my stride meaningful, my attention unwavering.

I don't say goodbye to Grandma, and nor do I acknowledge any of the guests looking to congratulate me on my toast. I stare straight ahead until I am out. Free.

I continue to walk—down the stairs to the foyer and then, my heels clipping noisily, across it. I am conscious only of my own breath, my own footsteps, until I reach the glass doors and wait. And wait.

Not for long. Not even a full minute in reality.

He doesn't speak. His hand on the small of my back is warm and intimate and my stomach dips. My knees almost buckle.

He guides me out of The Ritz and I smile at Hughes. I am prepared to step apart from Jack, to put some distance between us. But he doesn't let me. His hand stays glued to the base of my spine, and the moment I step into the limousine he catches my shoulder and spins me.

His eyes are charged with emotion, but I cannot fathom what he's feeling. I know only that he wants me with the same burning desperation that rips through me.

'We're going?' I prompt, my eyebrows raised.

'You'd better fucking believe it.'

And then, as if he has no choice, no free will, no say in the matter, he drops his head and presses a bone-meltingly lovely kiss against the tip of my nose.

As if I didn't love him enough already.

CHAPTER TWELVE

'CARRIE?'

My voice is croaky and my eyes sting as I answer my phone. I'm tired. What bloody time is it?

I peer into the darkness of Jack's room and panic sets in.

I've slept in his bed. With him. All night.

Or have I? He's not in the space beside me and his pillow is cool to the touch.

I look beyond it to the clock on his bedside. It's not as early as I feared—just gone eight. But it *is* Sunday, and I probably only got an hour's sleep the night before.

My cheeks flush pink as I remember the way our bodies rediscovered one another. Desperate at first, we came together as soon as we walked in the door of his apartment. Then slower, more sensually. An exploration. A reacquaintance. And finally dominatingly, Jack using my needs to control me and me letting him, loving it.

Still, I realise I haven't spoken to my friend in weeks, since our rescheduled catch-up. 'Is everything okay?' I ask.

'Um, shouldn't I be asking *you* that?'

'Why?'

I frown, running a finger over the crisp white duvet. *Where's Jack?*

'What's up?'

'I take it you haven't seen the papers yet?'

I shake my head, scrambling to remember which of Jack's business deals was at a crucial stage. What could have gone wrong?

Cursing under my breath, I find my feet are half-way to the ground when Carrie reads aloud: *"'Beauty and the Billionaire...'"*

Oh, shit.

'What is it?'

'Want me to read it?'

'Give me the gist,' I murmur urgently, dipping my head forward.

"'Renowned billionaire philanthropist and widower Jack Grant may be ready to get back into the swing of things. Spotted out and about with Lady Gemma Picton at The Ritz last night, blah-blah-blah...'" Carrie says under her breath, and then resumes reading. "'The pair have worked together for some years, but it appears their relationship has moved to the next level. Is it possible Britain's favourite billionaire is about to be taken off the market?'" She pauses, letting the words sink in. 'There's some photos, too.'

'I'll bet there is.'

I stand, reaching for Jack's robe, which hangs on the back of his door. It's dark blue towelling and falls all the way to the floor on me. It smells like him; my senses respond predictably.

'Which paper?' I cinch the robe tightly around my waist, my hand on the doorknob.

'The *Daily Gazette*.'

'Oh, well,' I say with relief. 'That's okay. What the hell are you doing reading *that*?'

'My cousin emailed it to me. She knows we're friends.'

'Great. But no one else I know will read it.'

'Sorry, mate. It's in the *Telegraph*, too.'

My eyes sweep shut. 'Shit.'

'Is it true?'

There's earnest concern in Carrie's voice.

My denial is as swift as it is untrue. 'No.'

'You guys look pretty cosy in the picture…' she says softly.

'Pictures lie. Look, I'll… Let me get back to you, okay?'

I disconnect the call before she answers, wrenching the door open.

Jack is fully dressed, a cup of coffee cradled in his hands, his attention focussed on the view of London revealed by the windows of his apartment.

Several newspapers sit on the table. I move towards them, instead of him, and cringe when I see that one of them has given us a whole page spread. Photos of us separately and photos of us working together make it look as though this has been going on for a long time.

And, yes, there's the obligatory photo of Jack and Lucy, taken on their wedding day. I'm drawn to her eyes, her smile, her kindness that shines through the picture.

There we all are—the three of us, together in print media for posterity, for anyone who cares to look us up in the future.

'I'm sorry,' I say softly, though I don't know what I'm apologising for, exactly.

'Why?' He turns around, a muscle throbbing in his jaw.

He looks both incredibly handsome and utterly awful at the same time. His skin is ashen beneath his tan.

'This—' he jerks his head towards the papers '—isn't your fault.'

'I know…' I shake my head slowly from side to side. 'But still…it's not ideal.'

His nod is curt agreement. 'I've left a message for Amber,' he murmurs, dragging the palm of his hand over his stubble. 'To explain.'

I nod. It makes sense that he'd want to give Lucy's sister the courtesy of a heads-up.

'Fucking paparazzi *scum*!' he says loudly, and he makes me jump when he slams his hand against the chair nearest to him. 'I wish they'd fuck off!'

'You're kind of famous,' I point out gently, and despite the palpable stress in the room my lips twist into an awkward smile.

But he's not in a joking mood. I sober.

'I guess my parents' thing…'

'I shouldn't have bloody come.'

The intensity of his reaction surprises me. I understand that he's upset; I am, too. This is invasive and unwelcome. And the timing couldn't be worse—just as we're finally morphing into something else, something perfect, we've been put in a position of needing to define what we are. But still…

'Jack.' I command his attention with a clear voice. 'This isn't the end of the world, is it?'

He stares at me, and I don't know if he's trying to work out why I don't get it or trying to calm himself down. But he doesn't speak.

I cannot make sense of this without caffeine—that much is certain. I move to the kitchen and fish a pod out of the canister, slip it in place. The whir of the coffee machine is the only noise in the cavernous apartment. I let it run through and then sip it, strangely pleased when it scalds my tongue.

'Jack?' I say again.

He's looking at me like he doesn't recognise me. A month ago this would have cowered me, but not now. Not after what we've shared.

'Damn it, Jack. You're freaking out for no reason. This is just a stupid gossip story. We can ignore it.'

'No reason?' he repeats, the words quiet but infused with angry disbelief. 'No *reason*?'

'Yes—no reason. So what? So what if you and I are seeing one another? Who cares? What's the big deal?'

'Jesus…' He spins away, his back to me, rigid as hell.

'I mean it.'

I take another sip of coffee, but when he continues to stare out of the window I slam the cup onto the marble benchtop, cross to him and grab his arm. I yank on it, drawing him around to face me. He's holding on—being CEO, cold, professional, unfeeling. But he's feeling *everything*. I know that now.

'We've been sleeping together for over a month. We had sex in Clint-bloody-Sheridan's home office. Did it never occur to you that some time, somehow, it would come out?'

'I never thought about it,' he dismisses. 'Or I sure as hell would have been more careful.'

I change tack, folding his admission into a part of

my brain that will later want to analyse all that is being said and done.

'*Why* is this a big deal?'

My eyes stare into his even as he looks away. I see every flicker of emotion on his face, and it's a little like watching a ship sink all the way from shore. I can't reach him. He's being devoured by an ocean that I cannot cross.

'Apart from the gross invasion of my privacy?'

I dismiss that immediately. 'You're a big boy and you're used to that. What else?'

'It's too much.' He shakes his head with weariness, running a hand over his stubbled jaw. 'Gemma, look… I have a thing this morning. I'm already running late.'

His sentence sits between us like a little row of tiny bombs. I can't help the look of disgust that crosses my face. 'A *thing*?' I ask, scorn deep in my tone.

'Yes, a thing. A breakfast.'

'You're *kidding* me?'

I lift a hand to his chest. He stands there for a moment, a tight smile stretched on his face, and then he steps back, dislodging my touch, breaking our contact.

His voice is coldly authoritative. 'Don't feel you need to rush off. You can let yourself out when you're ready. Hughes will…'

'*Fuck* Hughes!' I shout, moving behind him. 'You aren't getting rid of me like that. *God*, Jack! I have put up with this for long enough. You blowing hot and cold. You want me one second—then we fuck and you're nowhere to be seen.'

That same muscle twists in his face, and it might as well be a bullseye for how badly I want to slap it.

'So we were photographed leaving a party? So people think we're an item? Well, guess what? We *are*.'

He steps back as though I've given in to temptation and cracked my palm across his cheek.

'We're sleeping together. Working together. We know each other inside out. What's the big fucking *deal*?'

'I can't do this right now.'

The louder and more screechy I become, the calmer he seems. And that just makes me even angrier! It's like a horrible hamster wheel and I don't know how to get off.

'We have to talk,' I snap, my voice quivering like an arrow striking a tree.

'Yes, we do.'

It's a softly spoken confession that fills me with more fear than it does relief.

'But not now. I really do have a thing this morning, Gemma.'

But I know his diary, his movements, and I can't for the life of me remember a single entry for today.

'What? *What* thing?'

He looks away from me, guilty, and, *God*, I am fuming. Is he lying to me? To get rid of me? Is he so desperate to avoid having an adult conversation about what our relationship's become that he's inventing reasons to get rid of me?

Fine. I'd rather go than beg him to love me—which is what I feel like doing.

But just when I'm about to flounce off like a teenager in a strop, at the very last minute, he says, 'It's Lucy's birthday.'

Boom! The bombs explode and, predictably, I reel.

'I always have breakfast with Amber on Lucy's birthday. Given this—' he gestures with outrage towards the papers '—I think it would be in poor taste to be late.'

'It's Lucy's birthday...' I say with a nod, but inside my stomach is turning and my heart is shrivelling.

Had I noticed the glass before? My eyes find it easily now. A single Scotch glass on the edge of the table.

My eyes sweep shut.

He sleeps with women to forget Lucy. And that's what last night was.

Oh, God. *Oh, God.* Panic is like bile in my mouth.

'That's why you needed to see me last night,' I say thickly. 'It wasn't about me at all, was it?'

And I was so sure we were moving to another level—that he sought me out because he needed *me*. Because he missed me.

But it hadn't been that at all, had it? It was about Lucy. Always Lucy.

His eyes are swirling with anguish and emotion. But I don't care. I grab the belt of the robe and loosen it, pushing it off as I walk back into his bedroom. My clothes are strewn all over the place, where we flung them the night before, and they've landed haphazardly—the roadkill of our passion; the pathway to his penance.

I pull my dress on without bothering with underpants; my fingers tremble. He's standing in the doorway. I hear him before I see him, but I don't pause. I slide my shoes on.

'God! I'm such an idiot! You needed to *forget*. You needed to obliterate all your grief and whatever and *that's* why it had to be last night. Right?'

He doesn't answer my question, but mutters, 'Can this wait until tomorrow?'

Obviously it's just about the worst thing he can say.

I clench my teeth together and nod—because while I'm fuming I know better than to make any rash decisions.

'You're an asshole,' I mutter, pushing past him, taking satisfaction from the way my shoulder jams against his chest as I pass.

I stalk towards the front door but then change my mind and spin around, moving back towards him. My hand pushes at his chest and tears sparkle in my eyes. I push him and then I lift up on my tiptoes and I kiss him. *Hard.*

My mouth punishes him and I sob into the kiss, hating him, hating Lucy, hating it all so much but needing him to understand.

I rip myself away, my breath dragging ferociously from my lungs, my eyes whispering warm droplets from their corners.

'That is about *you* and *me*. Nothing else. No one else. It's *us*, Jack. Got it?'

He is infuriatingly immovable. His hands on his hips, his breathing even.

'Tomorrow,' he says softly, like a plea, and I nod.

But I know what tomorrow will bring.

Tomorrow is the dawning of a new day; tomorrow will be our end.

She is everywhere I look, despite the fact no visible sign remains. She's in the rumpled sheets of my bed, the towel I dry myself with after the shower, the toothbrush next to mine in the bathroom vanity unit. She's in the half-drunk coffee on the bench and the pool of coffee beside it, from where she presumably slammed it down.

I didn't noticed at the time but she must have been angry to do that. Gemma doesn't waste coffee.

My expression ghosts with a smile but I blank it.

I find myself standing in front of the newspapers once more and I look at Lucy. It's like I've been stabbed through my heart, a pain familiar to me. She was so happy on our wedding day; we both were. How could we have known what darkness was in store?

I press a finger into the page, as though I can touch Lucy's hair in real life if I press hard enough. But she's just a collection of black dots on cheap grey paper.

Fuck.

My finger moves to Gemma's face and lingers there, just beneath her chin. It's a larger photograph—almost half the page. The way she's looking at me... My gut twists and my throat aches.

Fuck.

The way *I'm* looking at *her*! How did I let it go this far? What madness has overtaken me?

I curl my fingers around the newspaper's edges and fold it back together, then collect them all into a stack that I carry to the wastepaper bin.

I get rid of them, and wish I could do the same to this mess.

I have to end it.

Gemma deserves better than this—to be jerked around by a man who can never give her what she wants. She wants my heart and it's no longer a part of me. I gave it to Lucy... She took it away with her.

The stars are not wanted now: put out every one;
Pack up the moon and dismantle the sun;
Pour away the ocean and sweep up the wood.

He's at my desk when I arrive the next day, looking immaculate in that blue shirt that makes me throb with the desire I partly want to cave in to. But I'm too angry, too sad, too hurt.

Grandma called me earlier, to enquire about my 'friend'. I didn't have the heart to tell her that the first 'friend' I'd had in years was about to put an end to things. Or that I was. That things had run their course.

'Coffee?' He nods to the mug in front of him.

I shake my head. I'm pretty sure I'll be ill if I eat or drink a thing.

'How was breakfast yesterday?' I ask, not meaning it to sound bitchy but suspecting it does.

'Fine.'

I'm pretty sure it *wasn't* fine, but Jack doesn't want to talk about it. And if Jack doesn't want to talk about it, then that's that.

I drop my handbag onto the floor with more force than is necessary and reach down, pulling out my Mac-Book case.

'I was blindsided by the press.'

'You and me both.' I move back to the door and click the lock in place.

'I've been careless. I shouldn't have let things go this far.'

'Bullshit,' I snap, a frown pulling at my whole face. 'Neither of us could stop this. It is what it is. We've worked together for two years—I *know* you. I'm not one of those women you bring home for a quick fuck.'

'You're not that,' he agrees, his eyes holding mine with an intensity that supercharges my blood. 'But there's no future for us.'

The words are spoken clinically, almost as though he's rehearsed them.

'Why not?' I'm not going to give in to my breaking heart and let him end this. Not just because he's afraid.

'This was never meant to be serious.' It's a short declaration.

'So? That doesn't change what we are.'

'Lucy—'

But I cut him off, shaking my head abruptly from side to side. 'Lucy and you... I don't want to infringe on that. I'm not asking you to renounce your love for her. I think you can love me, too. I think you can stay true to what she means to you and still make room for me.'

He clenches his jaw. 'I married Lucy for life.'

I nod slowly, my heart whimpering somewhere near my toes now. 'Even though she passed away?'

'Yes.'

He is so certain, so intractable.

I try a different approach. 'What would Lucy have wanted?'

He clears his throat and turns away from me. 'It doesn't matter.'

'I think it does,' I say with quiet determination. 'If you're going to invoke this woman as your reason for shutting this down, then I think you should at least pretend to consider what she would have wanted.'

'Lucy had only months to come to terms with her condition,' he says. 'She didn't grapple with how I'd live after she died.'

'Bullshit,' I dismiss angrily.

He's resigned. Frustrated. Tired. 'You didn't know her, Gemma.'

I move closer towards him, my voice a whisper. 'I know that anyone who has been in love would want their partner to be happy. Not to live out their life in a hollow, empty wasteland as some kind of sick tribute.'

He squares his shoulders as I speak, as though he can make my words bounce off. 'It doesn't matter.'

It's so arrogantly defeatist that I almost laugh. But I'm weary. So weary now. Deflation has set in and is sucking my energy.

'What are we *doing*, Jack?'

He turns to face me slowly. 'I've been asking myself that same question.'

'What do I mean to you?'

I look at him as he sweeps his eyes shut, the truth apparently not something he's ready to communicate to me.

'You're my in-house,' he says, with so much gentle concern that I feel tears sting the back of my throat. The use of my actual job title makes everything worse, somehow. 'And my lover.'

I am very still while his words sink in. 'You can't compartmentalise me. I can't be your employee at work, your lover after hours and nothing in between. It doesn't work like that.'

'Why not?' he demands with husky urgency. 'This is *good*. Those things are good.'

'But I want more.'

'That's all I have,' he says honestly. 'It's all I can give you.'

A muscle jerks in his jaw and I lift my finger to touch it lightly. 'You've already given me so much more. Don't you see that?' I say gently.

'It's not possible.'

His eyes are dead ahead, his jaw locked. I know Jack Grant—I understand him. I know when he's made his mind up and when it's useless to argue. I see his determination and in it is the answer I have been waiting for.

It is the end.

And yet knowing that and truly accepting it are two different things.

'How can you think this is just sex?'

He shakes his head. 'I should have been more careful. I'll never be what you want.'

'And what's that?' I push, approaching the precipice of what we are.

He meets my eyes; there is bleak reality in them. It breaks my heart.

He reaches for my hand and squeezes it. 'I'm not your boyfriend. I don't want to be. And I don't want us to get more serious. I just want to fuck you.'

Oh, God. The pain is like ten thousand blades running over my spine. It's unbearable and yet I revel in it, because somehow I feel I deserve it. It makes it easier to accept the truth.

My head jerks upwards. My eyes are clouded by grief. 'So that's it?'

His expression shows that he too understands the inevitability before us. 'Yes.'

His voice is pleasingly roughened by emotion so I know he's not unaffected.

I don't trust myself to speak. Not for a moment. I wait, counting to twenty in English, French and Russian, and then I reach into the neoprene case for my laptop and pull out the crisp white piece of paper I printed that morning.

'This is Carrie Johnson's CV. She'll be in at lunch-time to meet with you.'

He frowns, as if the sudden change in conversation has surprised him. As though he expected me to argue for longer, to fight for what we were.

'What for?' He doesn't look at the CV.

'For my job.'

A second passes while we both absorb the reality of that.

'She's excellent. Highly qualified. You'll like her.'

His face drains of all colour. 'What the *hell* are you talking about?'

'Obviously I can't continue to work for you,' I say with quiet determination, zipping my laptop case. My fingers are shaking, making a mockery of my calm delivery.

'Stop. That's bullshit, Gemma. Utter nonsense.'

'That you think so underscores why I need to leave.'

Fuck it. Tears are rolling down my cheeks now but I don't bother to check them. What does it matter?

I stuff the laptop into my handbag with relief.

'You've worked for me for two years. You can't just…because we…you *can't* quit this job. You can't quit on *me*.'

Quit on *him*? The nerve! *He's* the one who's quitting. I bite my tongue. More tears are stinging my throat and I don't want to indulge them.

'I can't work for you, Jack. Not for another minute.'

He's truly aghast. 'Why the fuck not? We're a team, aren't we?'

'Yeah. In bed. In the boardroom. But not in real life. No, thanks.'

He waves the résumé in the air. 'I don't want this…
Carrie Whoever.'

'You'll need someone, and she's got what it takes to
put up with you. She's got killer legs and a great rack.
You'll probably get her into bed in a week or so.'

Jealousy rings in the statement. I don't care about
that either.

'*Christ*, Gemma.' He drags a hand through his hair
and it spikes in a way that makes my stomach roll.
'Don't *do* that. You're making it seem like that's all
we were…'

'No. That's what *you* did,' I say angrily. 'You just
said it. We're lovers. We work together.'

He tilts his head back, a growl escaping his lips.
'At least stay for the week. Let's just let the dust settle
on all this…'

'I can't.'

I'm emphatic; my life depends on his acceptance
of this.

'Why not? It's just a week. Seven days.'

'It's so much more than that. It's all of me. It's my
heart. Don't you *get* it? This might have been just con-
venient sex for you, but to me… It's *everything*. I've
fallen in love with you, Jack. I love you completely.'

I wait. And a part of me waits in hope. In the desperate, unfounded hope that he will say it back. That
he feels it, too.

But he says nothing. He stares at me, and I stare at
him, and finally—well beyond the time I should have
given him—I lift my bag onto my shoulder and walk
out of my office. I keep my head bent and I don't even
acknowledge Hughes when I pass.

I'm so fucking *done*.

CHAPTER THIRTEEN

We need to talk.

THE MESSAGE BUZZES into my phone at three the next morning. I stare at it, my heart pounding, tears leaking out of my eyes. They make me angry.

I delete the message and turn my phone off.

When I wake up I've almost forgotten about it. I make my coffee, switch my phone on and it buzzes immediately.

Four messages from Jack.

You can't just ignore me.

I was surprised yesterday. I didn't handle it well.

Meet me for lunch today.

Please.

I turn my phone off again and leave it at home when I head out. After being tied to Jack—tied to my phone, my emails, my laptop—for the last two years, I'm looking up. Finally. And seeing.

I walk from Hampstead through Regent's Park to the British Museum. I don't think I've been in since I was a teenager, and strolling amongst the exhibits now gives me the perfect dose of perspective. Seeing the ancient Egyptian tombs, the mummies so perfectly preserved, the sarcophagi all shining and morbidly beautiful, I am reminded that I am just one person.

That Jack is just another.

That life is long and its adventures many.

I am philosophical enough to smile as I leave, but my heart is broken again when I walk past a man who is wearing something a little bit like Jack's aftershave.

Dejected, I head to my favourite restaurant in Dean Street and grab a counter spot, eating a roast lunch with a bucket of wine and staring out at the street as people pass.

A matinee show after that, and a slow walk home.

I'm exhausted when I finally get to my front door, and in no mood to see a huge bunch of ranunculus waiting on my step. I know they're from Jack without even looking at them, so I step over the arrangement, careful not to touch it with even the toe of my shoe.

I'll deal with them in the morning. When I have more energy. Hell, maybe I'll get lucky and someone will steal them to save me the hassle.

I stare at my phone as if it's a lit fuse. I'm torn between switching it on and throwing it in the bin.

It's cowardly, I know, but I leave it off. I send a quick email to my mother and grandmother, telling them I've lost my mobile and that they can contact me on email if there's an emergency and then I go to bed without eating dinner.

I'm too wrecked.

The next morning, I am woken by his knocking at the door.

I know it's him because who else knocks with their whole palm? As though they have a God-given right to disturb you whenever the hell it suits them?

I ignore him, but my throat is thick with more damned tears and my heart is spinning in my chest.

His voice is muffled but it speaks directly to my soul. Deep and dark. He's calling my name.

I burrow deeper under the duvet, pulling the pillow over my head.

I can still hear him swear loudly.

Finally, though, he's gone.

I stay in bed all day. I doze, and I stare at the wall, and then I doze some more. I have never been in love before, and I've certainly never had my heart broken. I have no concept if this is normal.

I feel as though I've been torn into a dozen pieces, ripped apart piece by piece, and as if my brain is too sluggish to remember how to rebuild me. Some time after dark my tummy groans. I'm hungry. That's a good sign, surely?

I shove my feet out of bed, grabbing a pashmina as I pass my wardrobe and wrapping it around my shoulders. I catch a glimpse of my reflection in the hallway mirror and grimace.

Pale face. Bed hair. Red-rimmed eyes. Puckered lips. *Ugh*.

I haven't grocery-shopped in days, but there's a pack of soup sachets in my pantry. I check the date on them warily. Only two months past, and surely there's enough sodium in these things to outlast a zombie apocalypse?

I tip the contents of one into a mug and stare at it while waiting for the kettle to boil.

It's a proverb, I know, so it shouldn't surprise me that it feels like I am waiting for ever, staring at the kettle, waiting for it to click off and signal that the water is hot enough. After several minutes I realise I haven't turned it on at the wall.

I curse under my breath and rectify the oversight. The kettle immediately spurts to life. I drum my fingers as I wait some more and finally, when I can hear it's near enough to boiling, I slosh a little water into the cup and whisk it noisily with a fork.

Halfway through the surprisingly *not* awful soup, I remember I told my mother I'd be available on email. I doubt she's tried to contact me, but I feel honour-bound at least to take a peek. I open my laptop and wait for the emails to come in.

Jack's I delete without reading.

Curiosity is burning in me, but I know he has nothing to say that will change what has happened. However he wants to make himself feel better, I won't allow it. He *did* hurt me. He *should* be sorry. It's not my job to assuage his guilt.

I force myself to concentrate on the other emails, to put Jack from my mind. There is one from Grandma and I smile weakly, imagining her typing it on the iPad I gave her for Christmas. It probably took her an hour.

Darling.
I'm worried. I can't explain it in any way that makes sense—I've had the heaviest feeling in my heart for days.
   I'm sure it's connected with you.

Can you call me tomorrow?
Gma Xx

My heart squeezes with affection for her. And the sense that she and I are connected in some way floods through me.

Trust Grandma to just 'know' when things aren't right in my world.

Everything's fine. But I'll call you tomorrow. Love.

I switch my computer off and finish the soup. I'm exhausted, but not sleepy. I've dozed all day, so I suppose that makes sense. I turn on the TV and stare at it for a few hours before going back to my nest.

I wake up with the sun, and only the thought of Jack coming again spurs me on to get out of bed. I doubt he'll be content to bang on my door a second time, and I don't particularly want to press charges for trespass.

I dress in running gear—for a quick getaway rather than any genuine interest in exercise—and pull the door open. The breeze slaps me in the face. I take care to step over the flowers, resolving to deal with them when I get back—really this time. I lock the door and begin to jog around the corner and up the narrow laneway that leads to several cafés.

Only I don't plan to stay in Hampstead. It's too close to Jack.

I catch a cab into Soho and lose myself in the throng of people and busyness. But as I kick out of Tottenham Court Road and get pulled into the riptide of shoppers on Oxford Street I have to stop walking and grip the brick wall beside me for support.

The pain is visceral and sharp.

The realisation that it's over—whatever we were, whatever it was—is deep and sudden. It ruptures my chest like barbed wire pulled at high speed.

I no longer want to be around people.

I move towards the road, lifting my hand and flagging down a cab. It pulls over on a double yellow, blocking a bus that lets us know its displeasure by sounding its horn loudly. I wave in acknowledgement and hurl myself into the back, giving my address and collapsing against the seat.

I must doze off because the cab driver speaks loudly as we arrive home and I'm startled as if from a deep sleep.

'Thank you.'

I tap my credit card and step out. It's early afternoon and my tummy groans with hunger. The breakfast I planned on didn't happen and I have only just realised. I step over the flowers once more, promising myself I'll throw them out soon, and push the door shut behind myself.

I've been home ten minutes when a knock sounds.

My heart thuds heavily.

I know it is Jack.

My eyes fly to the mirror opposite. I am still pale, but I brushed my hair this morning, and at least I'm dressed in something other than ill-fitting pyjamas.

'Open the door, Gemma.'

My heart twists. I have never doubted my strength in all my life, but now...I don't know if I can do this. Can I look at Jack, knowing I can't touch him? That it is over? That we are over?

'Gemma? I will stay here all goddamned day if I have to.'

I don't doubt the sincerity of his statement.

Sympathy for my neighbours has me wrenching the door inwards.

And the sight of him causes me to suck in a huge breath. Because he looks so much like *himself*—so strong and powerful, so confident, so *unaffected*—that any lingering hopes I've nurtured of his being as destroyed by this as me die an immediate, suffocating death.

He's staring at me. His dark eyes are haunting my face, dragging over my cheekbones, my lips, down to my throat and then back up again. He blinks as if to clear his thoughts.

'You're home.'

I frown, keeping my hand firmly tethered to the door, holding it in place as if my life depends on it. 'Yes.'

He bends down and lifts the flowers. A pool of dark brown has formed on one side of the waxed paper, where the overnight dew has set in. I look at the once-cheery blooms and am sorry for them. Sorry I gave them such a cold reception.

None of this is their fault.

I narrow my eyes, my heart pounding and breaking at the same time, like one enormous wrenching storm inside my chest. 'What do you want, Jack?'

I see his throat bob as he swallows, and I resist the urge to make this easier for him.

'May I come in?'

Just the question alone sets fire to my veins. It's so

unlike Jack that I am surprised enough to consider re-lenting. But I don't.

I have seen his dark places. All of them. And he has birthed new ones in me.

'No.'

Exasperation flickers on his face. 'I reacted badly the other day. I'm sorry.'

He did. But it doesn't change the facts. Perhaps at another time he might have found a softer way to let me down, but nothing will alter the truth. I love him completely, and when I told him he made it obvious he just wanted me to go.

The memories strengthen my spine and fire my de-termination.

'It's fine,' I say, even managing to dredge up a smile. 'Let's just chalk it up to life's experience and move on.'

He groans and shakes his head. 'I don't *want* to move on.'

'And yet you ended it.' I swallow, afraid I'm going to cry yet again.

'I didn't fucking *end* it.' His eyes are earnest as they meet mine. 'I didn't *mean* to end it.'

My heart screws down inside me. 'You freaked out when our story went into the papers.'

'It was Lucy's birthday,' he says softly. 'I think it's fair to say I wasn't in a good headspace.'

'That night...' I look over his shoulder, my throat thick and tasting acrid. 'You used me to forget her.' My eyes sweep shut. I can't bear this anymore. 'I thought you were there to see *me*.'

He takes advantage of my temporary weakness to push the door inwards, to catch my face with his hands and hold me steady, and then he kisses me as though his whole life has come down to this moment.

As though it is the most important thing he's ever done.

He kisses me with hot, fiery need and I sob in my throat as I kiss him back—but only for a second. And then my hands are on his chest, pushing him, and my back is against the wall, holding me upright as my breath is dragged out of me. He stares at me for a moment and then pushes the door shut. The flowers are discarded once more, but inside now, nestling against my shoes.

'You said you love me.'

He says it like a challenge. A cold line of truth that I can't take back.

'Yeah. I remember. I was there.'

His eyes narrow at my sarcastic retort. 'And? Is it true?'

I screw my face up and drop my head into my hands. 'Fuck you, Jack.'

He grabs me by the wrists, pulling my hands away so he can see my face, and he's so close that I take comfort from his body even when I know I shouldn't. When I know I should be demanding he get out of my house.

'Because I've been thinking about love, and how it's not something you can just walk out on.' He pauses, perhaps waiting for his words to sink in. 'You think you love me? Prove it.'

I suck in a breath and lift my eyes to his face. He's stroking my wrists, his strong legs straddling me. Without him and the wall I think I'd slide to the floor.

'Don't walk away from me.'

'Why should I stay?' I whisper, the words coloured

by a thousand shades of sadness. 'You told me in black-and-white terms there's no future. I can't be with you. I sure as hell can't *work* for you.'

He nods, but his hand lifts and strokes my cheek. 'When I met Lucy I fell in love with her straightaway.'

I spin my head away, twisting it to the side, hurting as though he's punched me in the gut. The pain is no less intense. I want to shove him away from me, but there's such earnestness in his voice, and I am obviously such a glutton for punishment that I stay, my mind absorbing the fact that the man I am hopelessly in love with is now telling me about his wife.

'But it was partly a selfish love. I loved her because she needed me. She made me feel like I was her entire world and I was addicted to that.'

His eyes hold mine, staring deep into my soul. I am exposed and self-conscious, because I find it hard to feel anything but resentment for his poor late wife.

'I wanted to save her. She needed me and I thought that was what love *was*. I didn't know it could be so different.'

The words form a crack. In my certainty and in my heart. 'What are you saying?'

'I feel like someone has cut inside me and excavated the very middle of my chest.' He grabs my hand and holds it against him. 'I'm empty *here*. I wake up and I can't believe I have to get through another day without you.'

His eyes probe mine deeper, deeper, watching and waiting.

'It's been three days. I can't do another one without you. I don't know when you became my reason for being, Gemma, but you *are*.'

Tears are burning my throat. I look away again, swallowing, hurting, *hoping*. But my brain won't let me be such a fool. Not again.

'It's just good sex,' I say stonily.

'I've *had* good sex,' he dismisses with deep-voiced urgency. 'I know the difference between that and what *we* are.'

My cheeks flush pink and I shake my head. 'You think that now because you didn't expect me to leave you. I *believe* you miss me. I believe you miss *fucking* me. I believe you miss me at work. But none of that is love.'

I force myself to meet his eyes and am instantly burned by the lie I've just told. Because I love him enough for both of us.

'How can you *say* that?'

It is a groan that perfectly echoes my own frustrations.

'How can *I* say it? *You're* the one who said it! And I think you spoke the truth. I think that's how you feel.'

'I was wrong. An idiot. I hadn't expected to love anyone ever again, and after two years you blew up my whole world. Everything I thought I knew and wanted exploded in front of me. I fucked up. *I fucked up.* I should *never* have let you walk away from me. I should never have let you quit.'

I swallow, my mind rushing to comprehend what he is saying, my brain working overtime trying to pick faults with his rationale.

'I don't believe you. You had so many chances to make this work. I think you can't stand that I've left you, but that's not the same as wanting this—us.'

'I wanted to convince myself that I could contain

our relationship. That we could be lovers and work together without any emotional fallout.'

I nod, and then I shiver. I realise belatedly that I haven't turned the heating on and the house is frozen.

'I know that. You did a great job. You were able to flick a switch and turn yourself off when it suited you. That's not love either.'

'No,' he groans. 'I couldn't. That's the problem. From the first time we kissed you have been all I can think about. That whole trip to Tokyo I was counting down the minutes till I could see you again. God, when you walked into the boardroom and you were so fucking *cold*—as though you could barely remember my name, let alone the fact I'd made you come against the wall of my office… Gemma…you've had me since then. I have been yours completely.'

A sob is silenced by my throat.

His voice is gravelly and I hear his sincerity, but my brain doesn't buy it.

'I'm messed up. I *know* that. What happened with Lucy was a shitstorm I never braced myself for. There are going to be days when I don't cope as well as others. Days when I am reminded of the tragedy of her loss.'

'I know that,' I whisper. 'That's natural.'

'Lucy's birthday—it's hard. It's a day that should be spent celebrating her chalking up another year and instead I just… I really feel her absence on those days.'

His eyes are bleak when they meet mine.

'The hardest part about realising I love you is accepting that I'll always feel like this. Like I'm betraying her by being with you.'

'No.' I shake my head, sadness for him filling me

up. 'I don't want that. I don't need you to choose between Lucy and me. We're different, and how you love us is different. You never have to hide that sadness from me. Don't you get it? I love *all* of you, Jack, and that means loving your grief and your sadness. Loving you even when you are lost and alone. Loving Lucy, too, and honouring your relationship.'

His eyes are wide, as though he has never imagined I could say that.

'She'd have been as pissed off as all hell at the way I've jerked you around,' he mutters. 'She'd have been glad I've fallen in love with you. She would have liked you.'

He strokes my cheek, his lips close to mine. So close. I breathe in deeply and can almost taste him.

'*I* like you,' he whispers against my mouth. 'I like the way you drink almost as much coffee as I do. I like the way you can't hold a tune to save your life. I like the way you don't put up with my bullshit. I like the way you use that magnificent brain of yours and make me exhausted just trying to keep up with you. I like the way you see me and know that beneath all the fucked-upness there's something about me that you actually like. That I'm worth loving.'

He is. He *is* worth loving, and I do completely. But it is all so complicated.

I bite down on my lip, staring at him through new eyes. 'I just don't… I braced myself for this to end. But for me it was never just sex.'

'No.' He cups my cheek, his smile a secret communication from his heart to mine. 'It was definitely never that.'

He kisses the tip of my nose, like he did after my parents' party, and as then my heart soars.

'I know there are no guarantees in life or love, Gemma. I know that better than anyone. But I'm not going to waste another second when we can be together. You mean too much to me. So? What do you say?'

'About what?' I ask, my lips twitching into a smile.

'Let's *do* this.'

'Do *what*?' I prompt, shaking my head slightly, feeling a sense of bemusement wrapping around me.

'Life. Together. You—me. For as long as we have. Never wasting a day or taking it for granted.' He pulls me into a bear hug. 'I want this. I want *you*—so much.'

I expel the breath I've probably been holding, in part, since I stormed out of my office three days earlier.

'Let's do this,' I agree, my smile stretching my face.

I have known happiness and sadness, but I have never known such perfect, utter rightness before. It settles into my heart and brings me peace and pleasure.

I am Gemma, he is Jack, and we have found each other at last.

EPILOGUE

'GEMMA? ARE YOU in here?'

Strange that in all the time I worked for Jack I never came to this side of his home. The mysterious 'Private Wing' of his mansion. And now I am here almost all the time—in his bedroom, his kitchen, his living room. We have barely been apart since that afternoon three weeks ago, when he came to my home and broke down all my defences.

'Yeah?'

I set down my laptop and stand, butterflies bouncing about in my stomach as though it is a forest and they its sole occupants.

He sweeps in and I hold my breath—as always, bowled over by his physical perfection. In dark jeans and a simple white T-shirt he is hypermasculine and edibly delicious. The idea fans my stomach and I'm walking towards him before I realise it, itching to touch him, to taste him.

He sees the intent in my eyes and chuckles. 'Wait until you've heard me out!'

But he pulls me to him, his hands seeking the hem of my shirt and lifting it so that he can hold my bare hips. He makes a small sound of relief at the contact and I echo it in my heart.

I understand.

This—being naked, touching—this is how we need to be.

'Remember my hunch about Ryan?'

It takes me a few seconds to remember the guy in Australia he didn't think would work out. 'Yes?'

His eyes are sparkling with something I don't understand. 'Well, it occurs to me that you would be an *excellent* candidate for his job.'

I blink, confusion and excitement at war within me. 'He's left?'

'Yeah. Just wasn't up to it. The job is difficult. I need someone I can trust.'

Of course the idea is instantly appealing. Building the Australian office from scratch would be a challenge to relish. And yet...

'It's a long way away,' I point out, as though perhaps my sexy, brilliant lover doesn't comprehend the logistics of geography.

'From London, yes. But we'd come back whenever you wanted.'

I freeze, my eyes flying to his face. 'We?'

A smile cracks over his face and I hold my breath.

'Why not?' He pulls at my top, lifting it over my head so that his hands can roam my bare back. 'Do you *really* think I'd let you move to Sydney without me?'

I stare at him and wonder if perhaps he's lost his mind a little bit. 'Jack...your business is *here*.'

'*I* am my business,' he says with a shrug. 'I can fly here whenever I need to. Fly people out to us. But I have it on good authority, my beautiful, distracting, brilliant Gemma, that you need to spread your wings before you settle down.'

'What?' I blink my eyes, realisation settling. 'Grandma?'

'Mmm...'

He drops his mouth, dragging his lips along my collarbone. I dig my fingers into his shirt front, a feeling of bliss spreading through me.

'She called me when she heard about our "developments".'

I laugh. 'That sounds about right.'

'She's given me a list of her requirements for when she comes to visit.'

'Oh, God.' I groan and laugh at the same time.

'I've told her she's welcome to come for as long as she wants. I think she's fancying a year or two in our guest room.'

I laugh and shake my head, but Jack leans closer, whispering, 'I've got an apartment downstairs. I think we'll set her up there so we can continue to enjoy our... *privacy.*'

I nod, grateful for his understanding. 'But, Jack, it's such a big move. Are you sure...?'

'Life's too short, Gem. You want to travel? To see the world? Let's do it. If we don't like it we'll come back.'

He lifts me up around the waist, carrying me easily to his bedroom.

His *real* bedroom. *Our* bedroom, I suppose, seeing as I have been with him here nonstop since the day he came to my house.

'Of course, if you need some extra convincing...'

I don't, but his lips around my nipple make speech impossible. I nod and murmur something incoherent, and as he kisses me until my body is vibrating and my insides are heated with need I see our future.

I see our home in Sydney, our love, and I fall apart in his arms, knowing that wherever we live happiness will surround us.

For as long as we both shall live.

* * * * *

LET'S TALK
Romance

For exclusive extracts, competitions
and special offers, find us online:

📘 facebook.com/millsandboon

📷 @millsandboonuk

🐦 @millsandboon

Or get in touch on 0844 844 1351*

For all the latest titles coming soon, visit
millsandboon.co.uk/nextmonth

*Calls cost 7p per minute plus your phone company's price per minute access charge